KEEP ME AT
Christmas

KEEP ME AT
Christmas

A ROMANO FAMILY ROMANCE

LUCINDA WHITNEY

Lange House Press

Edited by Michele Holmes and Emily Chambers
Cover design ©2018 Lange House Press
Layout and Formatting by LJP Creative
Published by Lange House Press

First Printing June 2018

ISBN-10: 1-944137-31-9
ISBN-13: 978-1-944137-31-1

*O melhor presente de Natal
é a presença de família envolta em amor.*

*The best gift at Christmas
is the presence of family wrapped in love.*

Romano Family

António
Teresa

- **Francisco**
  Mariana
  - Tiago
  - Catarina
  - Daniel
  - André

- **Luís**
  Glória
  - Matias

- **Carlos**
  Celestina
  - Jacinta

- **Manuel**
  Antónia
  - Filipe
  - Luciana
  - Paulo
  - Ricardo

- **Pedro**
  Adelina
  - Gabriela
  - Juliana
  - Alexandre

- **José**
  Patrícia
  - Nuno
  - Susana

- **Vicente**
  Ana Maria
  - Carlos
  - Pedro
  - Dinis
  - Anita

CHAPTER ONE

MONDAY, DECEMBER 11TH
HUDSON SPRINGS, NEW YORK.

Luciana Romano looked out the car's window. The first sunrays hadn't made their appearance, yet the small town was dressed in light and color. Christmas Day was two weeks away and she had never seen so many decorations and string lights. Even the car service she rode from the airport to the museum had a Santa Claus bobble-head perched on the dashboard. His fat rosy cheeks and perma-smile bobbed in time with his nodding head. The corner of her mouth rose as well.

She turned her attention back to the charming streets. She had worked in European museums before, but this was her first time in the United States, and the contrast was palpable. An altered kind of energy strummed through her—everything was different here, and she was ready to embrace the change and experience new things.

A soft gasp escaped her lips at the beautiful scenery and the appeal of the small town. Her lips upturned, unable to hold back the grin forming on her face. As the car rolled through Hudson Springs, Luciana's excitement grew. Any lingering doubts she had about this trip slowly fizzled out.

As the driver took her to her destination, more and more of the little town revealed itself. She would be spending Christmas here, away from her family for the first time. The Romanos always got together for the season, with very few exceptions. The guilt for leaving on business during the holiday season still gnawed at her more often than she wanted, but she'd needed to get away from all the wedding preparations. With two cousins getting married—one of them only three weeks away— bridal showers, wedding dress shopping trips, cake tasting, and venue visits were all inevitable, as were the happy sighs and starstruck eyes. Her cousins talking about the people they had fallen in love with was only natural. But as happy as she was for Catarina and Matias, there was only so much a single woman could take.

Was it jealousy? Maybe a little. Luciana wanted that kind of happiness for herself. She wanted a forever kind of love with a man who would love her with all his heart—someone who would feel like home to her. Because, right now, she was the odd woman out, the one without a pair. Loneliness was real.

Luciana settled a hand over her middle and pushed down the nerves. She had two weeks to finish a restoration job that someone else had started before getting sick. Her work day needed to start early—there wouldn't be much time for sightseeing. But coming to Hudson Springs was the distraction she'd needed. And the town was the most charming she'd ever seen.

"Wow," she said, wide eyed. "It's like a Christmas postcard."

The driver looked at her in the rear view mirror and smiled. "Indeed it is. Hudson Springs is famous for its obsession with all things Christmas. You've arrived right in the middle of the festival. How long are you staying for?"

"I'm leaving on December twenty-seventh in the late evening."

"You're going to love Christmas here," the man said with a definitive tone in his voice.

"I have no doubts." She already loved it.

Passing the season here involved in something she absolutely loved was the best cure for her lonely heart. Didn't Avó Teresa used to say that focusing on others' problems was a sure way to see your own in a better light? Luciana was here to help the Hudson Springs Museum finish readying the display, and that would keep her plenty busy.

The museum board had first contacted her in August, but at the time, she'd had too many other projects going on. She'd heard from them again on December fifth, begging her to take the project after their textile manager had stepped away on account of

3

sudden illness. By then, Luciana had been ready for a change, and she'd gladly accepted the invitation.

Her family hadn't been too happy about her leaving two weeks before Christmas, but this was one of those times when she had to do something for herself without long explanations. They wouldn't have understood her need to get away, and she hadn't wanted to deal with the guilt. She'd be back in time for Catarina's wedding, and by then she hoped she'd be feeling less morose.

The car came to a gentle stop in front of a two story building close to downtown. She'd researched Hudson Springs before leaving Lisbon, had looked it up on Google Maps, and she remembered the building from the photos, even if it was a little dark in the pre-morning light.

The excitement bubbled in her chest and she smiled again. Her first day of work in the new assignment awaited her. She found her wallet and paid for the fare, adding a tip.

"They won't be open for a couple hours or more," the driver said. "Are you sure you don't want me to drop you off somewhere else?"

Luciana hesitated. She rolled down the window halfway and peered at the building. Other than the Christmas lights decorating the outside, the inside was dark and locked. Her reservation at the local inn had a late check-in, since she'd planned to start with work first. This was what happened when she changed her flight reservations at the last minute—she'd arrived

4

in Hudson Springs too early. What was she going to do until then?

"Are you from around here?" she asked the man.

"Yes, I am." He smiled at her. "I pick up a lot of people from the airport for Mr. Garrison." He looked to be in his early forties.

Mr. Garrison owned the Hudson Springs Museum, but she had dealt with the curator through emails and phone calls, not the owner.

"Do you know of any good places that are open for breakfast?" She asked.

"I know just the place."

He weaved through a side street and turned onto Main Street where rows of one- and two-story buildings with store fronts lined up on both sides, most of them closed at this time of day. The whole street was merrily decorated in tones of green, gold, and red, and thousands of twinkle lights shone brightly.

Luciana stared for a few moments, her mouth opened. She had no other words.

"We decorate the whole town from December eighth until Epiphany. But wait until you see our festival. It starts on Thursday. Okay, here we are." He stopped in front of a building with a red awning. He exited the car, grabbed Luciana's luggage from the trunk, and placed it on the sidewalk. "Tell Jack DiLorenzo 'hi' from Frank."

"Thank you, Frank," Luciana replied.

She settled the small suitcase in front of her on the sidewalk and shouldered her large purse. As the cold nipped at her neck, she wound her knit scarf closer. DiLorenzo's ~ Italian Bakery and Café. The main door stood to the right and the front window spanned the width of the establishment. It looked promising and it smelled divine.

Her stomach rumbled, reminding her she hadn't eaten much since the night before.

Luciana pushed through the door. When she stepped inside, a wave of warmth enveloped her like a soft cashmere blanket, the sweet smell of baked goods adding to the contentment. Propping the suitcase next to her leg, she tugged off her knitted gloves and smiled, taking in the space before her.

Small round tables with marble tops dotted the floor, half of them filled with patrons, and a long wood bar flanked the side wall where customers stood in line. A refrigerated glass display followed the length next to the counter, all dark wood and shiny chrome. Pops of red, gold, and greenery dotted the room, and a small, decorated tree sat on a sideboard against the wall by the door. The layout reminded her of her favorite café in Lisbon, and she was instantly attracted to the European ambiance.

From the little she'd read online before leaving, the small town of Hudson Springs was proud of its heritage. The town history boasted a past full of English, Irish, and Italian immigrants. An Italian café blended right in. Maybe she'd be back again in the next few days.

She approached the counter and eyed her choices while she awaited her turn in line. A dark-haired man stood with his back to her at the espresso machine, and two ladies were busy fulfilling bakery orders and breakfast items. The family resemblance between the women was uncanny, the older woman clearly the mother of the younger one. They smiled and talked to most customers like they were old friends, and occasionally talked to each other in a language that sounded like Italian. Luciana smiled to herself. They reminded her of Avó Teresa and her aunts when they worked in the kitchen; even their facial expressions and behavior were similar.

The older lady approached and smiled. "Buon giorno. Welcome to DiLorenzo's. What can I get you this morning?"

Her English was heavily accented but otherwise clear to understand, and Luciana returned the cheery greeting. "Buon giorno."

The lady's smile widened and she replied in rapid Italian.

Luciana chuckled and shook her head. "I'm sorry. I really don't speak Italian."

"Ah, che pecatto. You look like you could be nice Italian girl."

The person behind her in line huffed impatiently, and Luciana looked back to the menu. She settled on a mushroom and spinach panini with Gouda cheese on a ciabatta roll, a chocolate pastry, and a tall capuccino.

The lady ringing her tab handed Luciana a plate with the pastry, and Luciana found a place to sit by the window. Her drink was ready within minutes and a college-age young woman brought it over.

Luciana removed her coat and scarf and sat back, sipping her cappuccino and taking little bites of the delicious pastry. She closed her eyes in appreciation of the rich flavors of the pastry and deep aroma of the drink, grateful for a few minutes to eat while she waited for the museum to open.

"Here's your breakfast," a deep voice said beside her.

It wasn't the young waitress. The tall, dark-haired man she'd seen before set down a plate with her warm sandwich. Like the others working at the café, he wore black jeans and a red shirt with the bakery's logo. He held her gaze for a moment and Luciana returned the eye contact. His smile was impersonal, almost practiced, but his dark brown eyes had a depth of expression that hinted to a strong personality. He looked to be in his early thirties, the kind of man she would like to sit down with for a long dinner and talk to into the night.

The thought surprised her.

"Thank you." She kept her gaze straight on him. "You must be Jack?"

His eyes widened. "How do you—?"

"Frank said to tell you 'hi'."

He kept watching her and cocked his head to the side, still holding her gaze.

He blinked. "Yeah, Frank. Of course." His shoulders relaxed, and he extended his hand toward her.

"I'm Jack DiLorenzo. Welcome."

Luciana shook his hand and when their fingers touched, Jack frowned slightly, which she hoped was more in surprise than displeasure. The contact sent tingles up her arm, and that was definitely unexpected. When was the last time shaking a man's hand had made her pause and think?

The two ladies appeared at his elbow, smiling, and the man looked sideways at them.

The younger one addressed Luciana. "Welcome to DiLorenzo's. I'm Paola. And you are?"

Luciana started to rise when they quickly took the seats around her, then gestured to her chair, and she sat back down. "My name's Luciana Romano."

The older woman grinned. "Ah, Romano is a good Italian name. Where are you from?"

"I'm from Portugal, but I'm not sure where the surname comes from." It did sound like an Italian name, as the lady said. It was possible Luciana's grandparents knew about the family name's origins; she'd have to ask them when she returned.

"If you're staying in town for a few days, you need to visit the festival," Paola said. "This is my mother Giovanna and Jack, my oldest."

The older lady smiled. "Jack can take you around and show you the festival. He knows it well."

Luciana glanced at Jack. He didn't agree to do it, but he didn't say he wouldn't do it either. His expression was rather neutral, as if he was used to being offered up for this kind of activity. Or maybe it wasn't the first time he was set up for unsuspecting dates with out-of-town women.

Just then a group of customers entered the café and made their way to the counter.

Jack's lips rose in a half-smile. "It was nice meeting you, Luciana."

"You too, Jack."

He nodded and returned to his position behind the counter.

Jack's mother, Paola, retrieved a pen from her apron pocket. "What's your phone number? Just in case."

Luciana eyed the pen. Paola's son probably wouldn't appreciate what his mother was doing, but it wouldn't hurt to give her number and accept the invitation. Luciana was only in town for a couple of weeks, and with such a charming place, she wouldn't say no to a cute guy showing her around.

She gave them her number, and they excused themselves when another group of customers came in through the door.

Luciana caught Jack once watching her from behind the counter, but he quickly averted his eyes. He didn't come out from his position again and instead called the young waiter to deliver the orders to the tables.

Once done with her food, Luciana stood and donned her wool coat, then shouldered her purse and grabbed the handle of her bag.

Paola waved at her. "Thank you for coming."

Luciana waved back and smiled. Just as she approached the door to leave, she glanced back and Jack turned to look at her at the same time. His expression relaxed and the corner of his mouth rose in a small smile. The exchange was brief, only a few seconds at most, but it happened nonetheless. And, as Luciana started walking back to the museum, it remained in her mind.

When she arrived at the staff entrance, an older man was waiting for her.

"Miss Romano?" The man extended his hand. "Welcome to the Hudson Springs Museum. I'm Augustus Wynthrop. I'm glad you could come to help us."

Luciana took his hand and smiled. "Mr. Wynthrop, thank you. I'm so glad to be here and finally meet you." They'd exchanged lots of emails in the month before.

This project excited her. She'd been hired to finish the restoration and make ready for exhibition a small collection of knitwear from the turn of the century.

She followed him to the back of the building, and he showed her to the room where she would be working. A row of large windows facing north covered one wall, with a high counter running beneath. Plenty of natural light and working surfaces. Perfect.

A young man approached from the corner.

"This is Oliver Kerrison," Mr. Wynthrop said. "He'll be your assistant for the duration of the project."

Oliver shook Luciana's hand. "Anything you need, Miss Romano, just let me know."

"Thank you. I will." She usually worked alone, but she wasn't opposed to having an assistant, especially with the scope of this project.

The morning went by too quickly. After being shown the textile collection in the room next to the workshop, Luciana spent time with each individual knit garment for a preliminary assessment of its current condition. This was a crucial part of her job. Rushing it would only result in mistakes she couldn't afford, costing extra time she didn't have.

The collection was not as large as she had anticipated. It contained women's shawls and fingerless gloves; baby bonnets and rompers; men's sweaters, cardigans, and socks. It was a practical assortment—a sample of utilitarian garments worn by immigrant working families in the late eighteen hundreds. The only exception was the inclusion of a beautiful bridal lace veil, knit with pure virgin white wool spun very thinly. It was the kind of piece to be the main attraction, and Luciana intended to give it the special honor it deserved in the exhibit.

The condition of the items varied by type and age, and some only needed a gentle wash and proper dry-blocking techniques. Others showed the passage of time, well-worn and well-loved as they were. Although the scope of the project was more manageable than what she thought it might be, the time-consuming tasks that each piece required wouldn't leave Luciana with much extra time for herself. Unfortunately, this was, often, a consequence over which she didn't have much control—traveling to exciting places and not being able to explore them.

Before leaving for lunch, she sat down to plan her list of special materials, supplies, and tools needed. She'd sent on ahead her small trunk that traveled with her to all assignments, and contained most of what she needed as far as tools. She hoped the rest would not be too hard to come by. Within minutes, the list was printed, and she passed it to Oliver, who hopefully would give it to the right people. Maybe she should take a tour after lunch and find out how many people worked there.

The museum was small, but Luciana had faith she'd have everything she asked for by the end of the day. The sooner she had it, the sooner she could start the work, and then return home in time for Catarina's wedding.

As picturesque as Hudson Springs was, nothing would hold her interest once she was done with the restoration work.

CHAPTER TWO

The bronze bell on the front door jingled, and Jack glanced up from the espresso machine.

She was back. The woman with the red coat and knit scarf. Luciana.

He looked away before she caught him watching her and filled the portafilter with coffee beans, distractedly putting it back. The familiar, strong scent filled the air. As she lined up to order, Jack brought his attention back to the ticket Mom had handed him a minute before. Two espressos, a latte, and a tall Americano.

Luciana had caught his eye as soon as she'd entered the café this morning. He hadn't seen her around before, and her smiling expression and bright eyes had grabbed his attention. The outside cold had brought a rosy hue to her cheeks, and the overall effect with her brown hair and dark eyes was lovely. She looked to be happy, confident, and at ease— everything he hadn't been in a long time.

After she ordered her panini, Mom had contrived to have him deliver it to her table. Not that Mom would admit to it, but Jack knew she'd done it somehow. He'd gone along with it, for no other reason than he lacked the will to protest. It was Monday morning, two weeks until Christmas, and he couldn't see anything different in his future.

His life was the perpetual hamster wheel—wake up and do the same thing as the day before, one day after the other, none of it according to his long-gone plans.

But today was different, and the change had come in the form of a foreign brunette, one who'd known his name.

His heart twitched in his chest like it had this morning when she'd said his name. The way she'd looked at him, with her smile and warm eyes, had jumpstarted something inside Jack—something he'd thought long dead. And he couldn't shake the feeling. What was more—he didn't want to shake it.

With each step she took closer to the counter, his chest warmed and his body thrummed as if in recognition of her. He kept focused on his tasks at the espresso machine, willing his heartbeat to calm down and his eyes to stay on what he was doing. What was he going to say to her?

Nonna beat him to it. "Ah, you come back. You liked breakfast?"

"I liked it very much," Luciana replied.

Jack turned around to the counter where he placed the beverages, and Mom handed him another ticket.

He looked at Luciana and the corner of her mouth rose. He nodded back at her. Did she remember how Mom and Nonna had offered him up to take her around? He should have said no right then.

"So now you want to try lunch?" Nonna asked.

"Yes, I do. Your menu looks delicious." Luciana looked up to the chalkboard on the wall behind him.

Her English was fluent, and he could only barely pick up her Portuguese accent. What had brought her to Hudson Springs? She didn't look like one of the skiers that came to the Mount Hudson Ski Resort. At least, she wasn't wearing any ski gear right now. His curiosity about her rose another notch.

Nonna kept chatting with Luciana as she ordered her lunch—a cup of the soup of the day, a small garden salad, and a half-sandwich, with a bottled water and a latte to drink— and rang her up. Like this morning, Luciana took one of the tables by the window, from where she could see both the outside, the front of the store, and the counter.

Jack set a glass and a bottle of water on a tray along with a napkin and flatware. Mom ladled the soup into a ceramic cup and placed it next to the bowl of salad. Instead of signaling his young cousin Liam, Mom picked up the tray and turned to Jack.

He raised his eyebrow at her. She was doing it again. His nephew Grant had called in sick and Jack had taken over making the sandwiches for him for today. As the head baker, Jack didn't spend too much time at the front of house anymore, and when he did, he preferred the espresso machine—not serving tables.

Mom matched his expression and placed the tray in his hands. Between Mom and Nonna, sometimes he didn't get a break from their matchmaking. He didn't argue with her; not in public. He'd have to talk to them again, in private, reminding them how he wasn't interested in dating, especially at Christmas time. Just because he'd exchanged a few words with Luciana didn't mean he was ready to date her, even if they had offered him up to show her around.

"I know what you're up to," he whispered when he passed his Mom. "Don't get any ideas."

She brought her hand to her collarbone and silently feigned innocence, but she couldn't fool him. Then she reached into the apron pocket and handed Jack a scrap of paper. "Before I forget, here's Luciana's phone number."

Jack stared dumbly for a moment. "Her what?"

Mom pushed the paper into Jack's apron pocket. "Her phone number. I got it this morning before she left. So you can show her around the festival." Then she gave him a little push. "Go on. She's waiting for her order."

Jack walked in Luciana's direction, his mind racing with what to say to her.

"Here you go." He placed the items on Luciana's table. "Your sandwich will be right out."

"Thank you, Jack." Her eyes were a soft brown, large and expressive. Smiling eyes.

He found himself smiling in return, unable to hold it back. "What's the verdict on the recommendation?"

"Excellent. I'll have to thank Frank if I meet him again."

Jack would too, and not just for recommending the café. He was obviously confused, wanting to get to know Luciana and knowing it wasn't a good idea. And then Mom had somehow gotten Luciana's phone number. "About the festival. When's a good time for you?"

Her expression softened. "Don't feel obligated to. I have a grandmother who likes to find dates for me all the time, so I know how that goes."

"You have a grandmother who likes to set you up with strangers?"

She chuckled, low and softly, and the sound of it tripped his heart again.

"I actually do," she said.

Maybe she did, but he wouldn't back out on it. Unless that was her way of letting him off. "If you don't want to, I understand. But I don't feel obligated." He held her gaze.

Something akin to curiosity and interest flashed in her eyes for a moment, and Jack found himself wishing she'd accept the invitation, despite all the warning bells in his head—loud and clear. It was his heart that urged him to jump in; apparently hearts didn't learn lessons as well as brains did.

He waited, but she didn't say anything, and his mixture of disappointment and regret surprised him.

19

He would have enjoyed getting to know her. "Enjoy your meal." He turned to go.

"Jack," she called after him in a soft voice and he stopped. "I just arrived in town today and I don't know how much free time I'll have. Can I let you know once I find out?" She grabbed her phone. "What's your number?"

Jack recited it to her and she entered it in her contacts.

"I'll text you when I know."

"Sounds good." He added a small smile to his words, hoping he hadn't come across as sounding too desperate.

This was the main reason he hadn't pursued dating anyone in the last two years. The uncertainty, the feeling he was playing a game he didn't quite know the rules for—it all took more emotional energy than what he had. Jack walked straight to the back room where he could take a breath without the stares of curious customers.

Luciana stayed for a little over half an hour, scribbling notes on a small pad. Not quite leisurely, but not rushing either. When Nonna approached to ask about the meal, Luciana put away the pen and paper, and they talked for a few minutes before she left.

Would she return tomorrow?

Jack pushed the curiosity away. It didn't matter if she did or not. He was too busy to think about an intriguing woman with a foreign accent and large, soulful eyes, even if he had been offered to serve as her guide and she'd sort of accepted.

Jack let out a low sigh. He was so out of practice.

After the lunch rush, the constant string of customers quieted down, and Jack helped cousin Ashley clean up. By the time they closed the doors at three in the afternoon, as they did each day, he was ready to sleep through the rest of the day until early the next morning. He climbed the back stairs to the second floor of the building, opened the door to his bedroom, removed his boots, and dropped into bed.

But sleep wouldn't come. Jack lay in bed, staring at the ceiling, his arms folded behind his head. When was the last time he'd given more than a quick thought to a woman he didn't even know?

He pushed her soft, brown eyes out of his mind and turned his thoughts to the product sheets awaiting him in the morning—the inventory of tasks and ingredients, the leftovers, the shipments, all the never-ending to-do lists. Christmas was one the busiest times of the year for them.

His entire life was a series of lists, one after another. How had he come to this point? As if he had the time to mope. This week, added to the everyday routine, he had to set up for the festival on Wednesday and finish decorating one thousand cookies for Friday.

Was he doing everything he ought to? Running the café, making sure Mom and Nonna didn't work too much, being available to his neighbors and Dad's friends, who were getting on in years. His sisters were busy with their own families and didn't need him anymore, although he still thought about them.

Jack rubbed his eyes and breathed out deeply.

Life had been simpler when Dad was alive. Dad and Grandpa had run a good operation at the café, even though Jack didn't remember his Nonno well anymore.

He'd been only seven years old when Nonno passed away, and his memories weren't clear. Dad had been gone for almost six years now. That, he remembered well. At times, Jack still expected to see Dad in the bakery in the early morning, rolling the dough on the marble slab.

Somehow, the family had made the transition. Both times they'd survived the loss; both times they kept plugging along. At least, where the café was concerned, they had made it. If only the rest were as easy.

Jack had been a few months away from graduating with his accounting degree when Dad died. It had been a shock to everyone—a massive heart attack. Jack had come home from the University of California for the funeral and then had gone back to finish the semester and graduate. But nothing was the same after that, and instead of following his plans to seek employment in San Francisco, he ended up returning to Hudson Springs to help Mom and Nonna run the café.

Six years—gone like that.

Jack gave himself a mental shake and rolled onto his side, closing his eyes. His priority was to rest, not wonder what could have been, and certainly not daydream about a beautiful woman who wouldn't be in town for too long.

CHAPTER THREE

When Luciana arrived at the inn's breakfast room the next morning, two young waiters were in the process of cleaning away all the tables in the room. The River View Inn wasn't the only hotel in town, but it was the closest to the museum. It was small by most standards—a three-story building dating back to the late nineteenth century. Just like all the other buildings she'd seen since arriving in town, it was extensively decorated for the season: lighted garlands and wreaths; Christmas trees of various sizes in the public rooms; and fresh greenery, red bows, and gold ornaments filled the walls, banisters, mantels, and any corner of space available. The effect was both impressive and overwhelming.

"Good morning, Miss Romano."

Luciana turned to the voice at her side. Mrs. Wells, the older lady who'd been at the check-in desk on

Monday evening smiled at her. Luciana smiled back. "Good morning, Mrs. Wells."

"Come with me," Mrs. Wells said. "I'll set a table for you."

Luciana followed the lady to a table by the window. Mrs. Wells pulled a place setting from an open shelf on the sideboard and set the items on the table.

"Excuse our slowness this morning. There's a filming crew from the Wedding Belles Channel in town, and all of them have breakfast at the same time." She filled one of the glasses with water.

"The what channel?" Luciana asked.

"It's a TV channel all about weddings." Mrs. Wells placed the butter and jams on the table, individual portions in small plates and jars. "They're doing a spotlight about the Mount Hudson Ski Resort as a wedding destination and came to town to film the festival since everything is decorated for Christmas. It's all very exciting, of course." She added a small pitcher of water to the array. "What would you like to drink this morning? We have fruit juice, milk, tea, and coffee."

Luciana gestured to the sideboard. "I can help myself to whatever is out." She motioned to stand, but Mrs. Wells pushed gently on her shoulder.

"Nonsense. I'll bring your breakfast out." Without waiting for Luciana's reply, Mrs. Wells brought orange juice and milk. "The filming crew had the buffet— there's so many of them, I can't serve them all at once."

The lady went on for the next fifteen minutes. She

laid a full breakfast spread for Luciana, all the while chatting about the upcoming Christmas festival and how many people came to attend it from the neighboring towns, and what a grand event it was—telling Luciana several times she needed to go.

As nice as it all was, maybe tomorrow Luciana would come down earlier for breakfast and join the filming crew for the buffet. She couldn't very well afford the time for a lavish breakfast every morning. For the moment, she kept quiet, not wanting to hurt the old lady's feelings.

Luciana arrived at the museum twenty minutes behind what she'd planned. She hung up her coat behind the door and unwound her scarf. "I'm so sorry I'm late. The lady at the inn—"

Oliver chuckled. "Mrs. Wells. She loves feeding her guests." He set a disposable coffee cup on Luciana's desk.

"You know her?"

He nodded. "Everybody does. She's a sweetheart but can chat up a storm, if you let her."

Luciana eyed the cup. "What's this?"

"Coffee from DiLorenzo's."

"Oh, bless you." She picked it up and took a sip. "That place has the best coffee."

"If you let me know what you like, I'll bring it tomorrow."

"Good manners say I shouldn't let you, but the coffee at the inn ..." She shook her head. "The food was awesome though."

This time Oliver laughed. "That's about right. Bad coffee and good food." He walked to the small desk in the corner and grabbed a binder. "I printed the notes from yesterday and made a checklist of the materials and tools you requested." He set the folder on Luciana's desk, then opened it to the first page. "The ones that have arrived have a check beside them."

Luciana glanced at the page and then at the young man in front of her. "I'm really glad I agreed to having an assistant. You're going to spoil me for my next job. I usually work alone." She'd had an assistant once in Berlin, and the experience had not been a completely positive one.

Red spots colored Oliver's cheeks. He looked young, at least five years younger than her own twenty-eight years.

"What got you interested in this project?" Luciana asked.

Oliver followed her to the workstation in the center of the room. "I'm familiar with your work, Miss Romano. I volunteered to be your assistant."

Luciana smiled. "Well, I'm flattered. I'm glad you enjoy textiles as much as I do." The assistant in Berlin had not volunteered. She'd been assigned to work with Luciana, and it had shown. By the end of the project, the woman's dislike of textiles had been too obvious to ignore. That had been one experience Luciana didn't want to see repeated.

She leafed through the rest of the pages in the binder. Each knitted piece had a section. "Let's start the in-depth assessment. We need a complete list of texture and color samples finished today."

From the little she knew, the first specialist the museum had hired had fallen ill before showing up for the job. Luciana was starting from scratch. Some yarns would be easier to procure than others, and with only two weeks to complete the project, Luciana worried for the hard-to-match pieces.

They worked steadily through the rest of the morning. Oliver and Luciana appraised and catalogued fifty assorted socks and nineteen matched pairs, baby rompers and bonnets, and fingerless gloves in a variety of sizes and styles—from men's work gloves to lady's Sunday best.

Some of the pieces had ribbon tags, usually of grosgrain or muslin, and Luciana photographed them so she could later type the captions to be displayed beside their corresponding pieces. It made the showing more interesting when the provenance, signature, and dedication printed or embroidered on each tag, accompanied the knitted piece it belonged to, but usually the handwriting was hard to make out, and the printed tags made more sense. The majority of sweaters and shawls would require more time and attention, so she and Oliver concentrated on the smaller, simpler pieces first.

Oliver photographed each piece, and Luciana collected samples for the collection binder and for the materials and source binder. Under a microscope, Luciana identified the color and type of yarn and registered them alongside the provenance.

Mr. Wynthrop entered the room. "Miss Romano, you do know you have an hour for lunch, right?"

Luciana looked at the clock on the wall. They'd been working for almost six hours straight. She stood and tapped her feet on the ground to restart circulation. "I didn't realize it was lunchtime already," she said. She pulled a sheet from the binder. "I have the museum's floor plan, but I'd still like to look at the room where the exhibit will be placed."

"How about we do that after lunch?" Mr. Wynthrop said. "I'll take you on a tour of the building and show you everything."

Oliver grabbed his jacket and excused himself, leaving quickly. Mr. Wynthrop soon followed. Luciana's stomach rumbled, and she set a hand over her middle. Lunch was beginning to sound better and better. She secured the samples and closed the binders, then put on her pea coat and scarf.

Mrs. Wells had given her a town map showing the restaurants, but Luciana already knew where she was going for lunch.

Luciana was here. For the second day in a row.

Jack had been watching the door all morning, waiting for her to come to the café. He'd told himself that it didn't matter if he never saw her again, but that was a lie. He'd hoped she'd return around the same time as the day before, and when the hour came and went without her showing, he pushed all thoughts of her aside. The busyness at the café on Tuesday morning and the preparations for the festival kept him working at a fast pace and with little time to wonder why she hadn't texted yet.

When she walked through the door at the lunch hour, the rush was in full swing. Jack peeked at her from his spot at the counter in the galley, and then went back to slicing bread. The corner of his mouth pulled up, but he reined in his smile, not wanting any attention from Mom and Nonna. He chided himself. So Luciana had returned. In a small town like Hudson Springs, outsiders who were not skiers stood out. By the end of the week, when the Christmas Festival was in full swing, there would be too many people in town to notice.

But Jack had noticed Luciana from the first time he'd seen her.

He grabbed two more loaves from the rack. She looked at the chalkboard, where the specials of the day were written. Her brown eyes were shiny, and her nose and cheeks flushed from the cold—just like the first time she'd caught his attention.

When she saw him across the way, her expression bloomed in a wide smile. Jack's chest squeezed, and he paused. What would it be like to experience that reaction and smile every day?

He willed himself to calm down from the nervous energy that momentarily surged through him. From the corner of his eye, he saw Mom sidle up to Nonna and elbow her in the side. They were on to him, and there would be explaining to do later. He ignored them pointedly and came from the kitchen to take Luciana's order.

"Hi. You're back.," he said with a smile. So original.

She smiled at him, and nodded. "Hi, Jack."

The doorbell jingled and three customers came in. Jack hid his annoyance. With all the interruptions and work he had to do, there was no way he'd have a chance to exchange more than a few words with Luciana. Of course, admitting to himself how truly interested he was in her didn't help keep the jitters at bay.

She followed his gaze to the front door, then turned back to him. "Are you always this busy?"

Jack chuckled, unable to stop himself. "A lot of skiers prefer to stay in town, but we get even busier during the festival."

As the line grew behind her, she shrugged a little. "I'm stalling the line. Sorry." She gave him her order.

Jack smiled again. "Don't worry about it," he said as she moved down the line to pay.

He cringed inside. He was so not used to this—what was it anyway? Flirting? Chatting up a pretty woman so he could invite her out? He kind of had done that already and was still waiting for her reply. Did he really want to go out with her? He hadn't even been out on a date in some time, not after his disastrous past.

Luciana looked around until she found a place at the end of the bar, then looked up to meet his eyes once more.

That feeling again. Like a stutter in his heart.

He was in so much trouble and totally unprepared for it.

A few minutes later he grabbed the tray from his mom's hands.

She raised an eyebrow at him. "I thought you didn't want to wait the tables."

Jack lifted a shoulder and winked at her. "It's the counter, not a table."

He approached Luciana. "Here we go. The cinnamon chocolate cappuccino, the breakfast pizza, the *pane del giorno* with the cheese and fruit spread of the day, and a sparkling water. *Buon appetito.*"

She was reading a small leather book and put it down when he placed the cup and plate in front of her.

"Thank you." She smiled up at him. "This looks fabulous."

"You're welcome."

Before he did something stupid, like ask about her work schedule, Jack walked back to the kitchen and pulled out the list for the festival, trying to keep busy and away from the front of the café.

He went through the freezers and recounted the trays of cookies for Friday at the festival, then went through the fridge to check the labels on the bags of frosting. Some of the cookies were old Italian recipes and required minimum assembly—just defrosting. Only the *pizelle* needed to be made fresh. In fact, they'd have a pizelle iron on Friday to make the traditional flat lace cookies. They were always a hit with festival goers, young and old.

Would Luciana be able to come? He didn't even know what she was doing in Hudson Springs. Why had he been flirting with her? However long and whatever reason she was in town for, it was likely her stay was very short. Did he really want to get involved with a woman who wasn't staying? Or did the fact that she wasn't staying for long make it easier to go out with her?

Of course, being new in town, she probably wouldn't want to go out with him once she heard about his past. Maybe it was a better idea to not flirt with her and disappoint her expectations. After all, he had not dated in a while for a very good reason. It would serve him well to remember that.

"Jack, your mom wants you," Ashley called at him.

Jack raised his head from the festival map on the counter and looked across the opening between the galley and the café. At the end of the bar stood Mom, Nonna, and Luciana. Nonna said something and the three women turned toward him. Luciana's smile was uncertain and Mom motioned him over. When he just stood there, Nonna mouthed *presto*.

A flash of clarity rushed through his mind. They had cornered Luciana to take the tour of the festival. He recognized their smug expressions.

He walked over to them.

"Luciana's in town for two weeks working at the museum," Mom said when he approached.

Only two weeks then. "Are you staying through Christmas?" he asked.

Luciana nodded. "Yes, I'm leaving on the twenty-seventh."

Jack nodded back then caught himself. Did she not mind being away from her family at this time of year?

Mom went on. "She has some time to look around on Friday."

Luciana looked away for a brief moment, but Nonna nodded and smiled.

Mom and Nonna wouldn't let it go, even if he wasn't ready to date. This wasn't a good time of the year for him—the second anniversary of his breakup with Madison. Something more than a breakup, but he didn't like to think about it too much. Last year he'd stayed away from everything to do with the season, and Mom and Nonna had let him alone. No such luck this year.

But if Luciana was only in town for two weeks, couldn't this be his chance to get his family off his back about dating? Even his younger sisters had started making not-so veiled comments about it, and it wore him out. Fifteen days were too short a period to develop any real feelings for someone, even if his heart somersaulted each time he laid eyes on her. He could take Luciana out on a couple of dates, play the perfect local host, and have a good time while at it.

Couldn't he?

Nonna touched his arm. "We were telling Luciana how Fridays are the best days at the festival."

Nonna said *Luciana* in Italian, with the hard *ch* sound instead of the soft *c* sound Luciana had used when she'd introduced herself. It was *Luceeana*, not *Luch'ana*, but if he pointed it out, it would get awkward really fast.

"Fridays are great days," he said at last.

The three women raised their eyes to him with mixed expressions on their faces, from relief to mild surprise, and even a bit of doubt, this from Luciana.

Jack scrambled for something to say. "Do you like cookies?" Seriously? His brain couldn't come up with anything better to say?

When a group of customers entered the café, Mom and Nonna excused themselves and left to attend the newcomers, leaving Jack and Luciana by themselves.

Hesitation flashed in Luciana's eyes, then she reached in her purse and handed him a business card. "Sorry, I gotta run. I'll be at the museum until six."

She was out the door before he had a chance to respond.

Jack glanced at the card. It simply said *Luciana Romano, Knits and Textiles*, followed by a phone number.

He had her number. Again; this time directly from her. She had his but hadn't used it yet. The situation was turning more awkward every time they met. Maybe it was up to him to take the next step.

He slipped the card into his pocket, hoping this wouldn't turn into another mistake.

CHAPTER FOUR

$\mathcal{J}$ack hadn't slept well again. Not sleeping well was nothing new, but the source of the problem was.

Luciana. Just her name made him pause and turn all his thoughts to her. It was a soft, happy name, just like she was.

He'd meant to set his alarm so he could wake up and call Luciana in the evening, but he'd been so tired that he must have slept through it. By the time he woke up, it was two in the morning. Although he didn't have to get up quite that early, he ended up in the kitchen and finished decorating the cookies for the three days of the festival.

In the meantime, setting up the booth gave him the time he needed to think.

Jack couldn't remember a time when the café hadn't participated in the town's festivities. As a child, he'd come with Dad to set up, and before he was old enough to help bake cookies, he'd been in charge of handing out the napkins and spoons.

In the past few years, since taking more of the baking responsibilities, he'd been training some of the younger cousins for the duties of setting up and taking down, making and serving the hot chocolate, and selling the cookies. Jack preferred to stay at the café's kitchen, rolling new batches of dough rather than dealing with the hordes of happy festival goers.

As one of the oldest businesses in town, DiLorenzo's had a booth across from the stage where Santa Claus sat, the most popular spot of the season. It was a good location that brought lots of business.

Today, Liam and Gavin were on duty assisting Jack with the wood panels. For the rest of the festival, the DiLorenzo and the Barisone families had a schedule of two people at all times rotating every two hours. Even with temporary electricity and heating, the outdoor paneled booths got cold really fast. The café was a popular spot, and their booth occupied a double space.

Liam held the first of the side panels while Jack used the cordless drill to secure the sides with screws. Around them, some of the booths had already finished setting up and had started decorating, and others were barely getting their walls and roofs up.

The day was sunny and cold, and being outdoors was a welcome change to the warmth and humidity of the kitchen where he usually worked.

Methodically, Jack handed the screws to Liam

while he shored up the panels that made the sides and roof of their booth. As he stepped onto the path to reach for a fallen bag of screws for the next section, he turned to find Luciana walking in front of their booth space.

She paused when she saw him. "Hi, Jack." She gave him a hesitant smile, then resumed walking.

"Luciana, wait," Jack said.

She slowed down and looked back over her shoulder. "I'm on my way back to the museum."

Jack handed the drill to Liam. "I'll be right back." His cousins knew what to do. It wasn't the first time they'd helped setting up the booth for the festival.

Luciana kept walking even as he caught up to her.

"I meant to text you yesterday," he said.

"Don't worry about it." She waved her hand to encompass the town square. "So is all this part of the festival?" she asked.

Instead of walking around the square on the sidewalk, they cut through the center, right in the middle of all the preparations. "You've heard about the festival?" Jack asked in a playful tone.

Luciana smile. "It's kind of hard not to. Everyone is talking about it. At the inn, at the museum, even at your café." She gestured to the row of stores closer to where they stood. "I've never seen so many Christmas decorations."

"Yeah, Hudson Springs is a bit obsessed with everything the season has to offer." Sometimes, it was hard to explain to the out-of-towners why this small town in upstate New York put so much effort in bringing out all the best of Christmas. "The town starts decorating on December eighth, which is also a holiday: the Feast of the Immaculate Conception."

"We celebrate it in Portugal too." Luciana smiled.

"Hudson Springs had an influx of English, Irish, and Italian immigrants in the nineteenth century, and lots of traditions are rooted in the Catholic holidays." Jack's family was Italian on both sides, but he had lots of friends from English and Irish families. "The decorations come down right after Epiphany."

Luciana nodded. "King's Day on January sixth. What are the booths for?"

"This is the culmination of that Christmas obsession I mentioned earlier." He chuckled. "By tonight, the town square will be transformed into a Christmas village. There will be vendors with decorations and food, and lots of Christmas music."

"Sounds like fun."

"It is actually." He was too used to it. Having been raised here did that to some of the townspeople. "Part of what makes Hudson Springs special." He believed it, even if he took it for granted more than he should.

"I'll have to come by and see what it looks like tomorrow," Luciana said.

"You should. If you like Christmas, you'll love it." As jaded as he might feel, Jack liked to see the looks on children's and visitors' faces.

"I come from a big family, and we always try to get together for the holiday season."

"A big family, huh?" Most people's families were not big, compared to his. "How big are we talking about?"

Luciana's eyes gleamed with amusement. "My grandparents had seven sons. Those sons married and produced nineteen grandchildren—cousins who are close enough to feel like siblings, adding to the three brothers I already have. I imagine the great-grandchildren starting to come now. Total chaos."

Jack let out a low whistle. "So you do understand about big families."

"More than you think," Luciana said. "Two of the cousins I grew up with are getting married next year, starting with one on New Year's Day. Another cousin will soon be engaged, according to family rumors. I called my grandmother before I left Lisbon, and she said in passing that I need to start looking at wedding gowns."

"Congratulations on your engagement," Jack said as he turned the information in his mind. He glanced at her left hand, but didn't see a ring. Did they hold the same traditions in Portugal?

Luciana shook her head and held her right hand up for him to see. "Not engaged."

He frowned at her and slowed down.

"I'm not even in a relationship." This time, Luciana chuckled.

"So, your family—" Jack started.

"My family is just like yours," Luciana finished. "Full of good intentions and always meddling." She stopped and looked at him. "Not that I'm saying your family is meddling. Sorry."

Jack laughed. "No, they totally are. And it sounds like yours is too."

She nodded again. "I could see what your mother and grandmother were trying to do yesterday. I'm sorry. I won't hold you to it, by the way."

She bit her lower lip, and, for a moment, Jack wanted to reach out and touch her. Did she think he was being coerced?

He slipped his hands in his pockets. "Christmas season is the busiest for us, especially with the festival this week, but not so busy that I can't show you around." He could skip a few hours of sleep. Going out with Luciana had moved to the top of his list. "Do you have plans for Friday evening?"

"I'm trying to finish a gift for my goddaughter, but nothing else going on."

"How about I pick you up at seven at the inn?"

She raised an eyebrow. "How did you know I'm staying there?"

"The motels are all located out of town, but since you're working at the museum, I figured you'd want to stay closer, and the inn seems like the logical option."

They'd walked to the museum and stopped on the sidewalk.

"Well, my lunch hour is over," Luciana said. "Oliver is probably back already, and we have a whole list of samples to finish."

"I hope you had the time to stop at the café for

lunch. I'm sure Mom and Nonna were happy to see you." If she hadn't walked by the booth, he'd have missed her too.

Luciana looked away for a moment, then shuffled in place. "I brought a sandwich. I didn't have much time today."

Was it lack of time or had she tried to avoid him because he hadn't texted her? This was the part he didn't like, the dating games and the expectations. Life was simpler when he didn't date. But also lonelier. He'd been so much more confident before Madison broke up with him.

He glanced at the front of the museum, where a large sign announced a new display coming soon. "What do you do exactly?"

"I'm a knit restoration specialist. I was hired to help restore and get ready for exhibition a collection of nineteenth century clothing items from Irish and Italian families from the area."

Jack raised an eyebrow and regarded Luciana. She was attractive and obviously smart and interesting. Anticipation coursed through him for their Friday night outing.

At his lack of reply, Luciana blushed. "I know. I have a weird job."

"No, nothing like that. I've just never heard anything like it before. I think it sounds fascinating," he said at last.

Luciana's cheeks turned even more red. She opened her mouth as if to say something, but the alarm of a nearby car went off and she turned toward the sound for a moment.

"I should go. Bye, Jack," she said.

Jack nodded as she pushed the heavy oak door and stepped inside.

He stayed for a little longer, replaying the past few minutes with Luciana.

She was an intriguing woman. In a way, he was relieved she was only passing through.

Otherwise, it would be a lot more complicated.

Luciana hung her coat and scarf on the rack. Oliver raised a hand in greeting, working at the photography station. She returned the greeting and approached her desk to look through the work binder.

The time she'd spent with Jack DiLorenzo was still on her mind. Was he the mysterious guy she'd shared a moment with when they first met on Monday, or the easy-going man she'd talked to today?

He'd let his mom and grandma set him up with a virtual stranger, but Luciana couldn't tell if he was used to it and didn't care enough to protest, or if he was interested in her. Or maybe he was just a nice guy willing to give a tour to someone from out of town, and Luciana was reading too much into it.

The impression she got of him was of a regular, genuine guy who loved his family and the place where he lived. She'd enjoyed their time together as they'd walked through the square and had seen all the preparations for the festival. So many preparations.

The little town of Hudson Springs was intriguing, as were its people.

One in particular.

Luciana sighed and put all thoughts of Jack away. She'd come to New York to work, not to meet men.

"Miss Romano, there's someone I'd like you to meet," Mr. Wynthrop said as he entered the room.

A tall, broad-shouldered man in a dark blue suit followed closely behind.

Luciana left the binder and took a few steps in their direction, curiosity rising.

Mr. Wynthrop stopped near the work station and indicated the man he'd brought with him. "This is Mr. Garrison, the museum owner. And this is Miss Luciana Romano."

"Pleased to meet you, Miss Romano." The man extended his hand to Luciana.

Luciana shook his hand. "Mr. Garrison, how nice to meet you. Call me Luciana."

"If you call me Matt." He smiled.

Matt Garrison was the kind of confident man who put others at ease. Luciana nodded and returned the smile. "I'm glad we have the chance to meet. I wanted to thank you for the chance to work on this project."

Even though Augustus Wynthrop had hired her, he'd told her about Matthew Garrison and his insistence that she be the one to restore the collection.

"I'm the one who should thank you for coming to our humble museum so close to the holidays. You came highly recommended, and it's an honor to have you."

Despite his flattering words, his manner was relaxed and his tone genuine, and Luciana felt a swell of pride that her work was appreciated this much.

"I'm passing through town and I was hoping to get a brief tour of what's been done so far," he said.

Would he not be here for the exhibit's début? Luciana held back her question. "Absolutely. Let me show you the plans and projections first."

Oliver rose from his station. "Good to see you, Matt."

Matt Garrison shook hands with Oliver. "You too, Oliver."

"I just realized you two have very similar last names. Are you related?" Luciana asked, curious at the possibility.

"Matt is from the English *Garrisons* and I'm from the Irish *Kerrisons*," Oliver replied.

Matt nodded. "We're practically cousins."

She looked between both of them. "Which name originated first?"

Both men chuckled. "That depends on which side you ask," Matt Garrison replied.

Luciana took him to the work tables and showed him the binder first, then she walked him through the different stations with all the steps in the restoration process, including the washing, the dry-blocking and mending, the pictures of the ribbon tags and the museum labels they'd started printing for each one, and the workroom that housed all the pieces in various stages—assessment, cleaning, and restoration. She ended the tour in the exhibit room where the supports for the displays had been brought in. Luciana pulled out her tablet and explained the projections and plans for the pieces and groupings.

"I'm so impressed with the work you're doing here," Matt said. "It'll be the best exhibit the museum has to offer, and I'm really excited about how much it will mean for the history of our town."

At his words, Luciana straightened to her full height. This was the second time he praised her work and she liked the recognition. Although she usually knew her clients appreciated what she did, the majority of them weren't always this liberal in sharing what they thought of it so directly. This man, in just five minutes, had made her feel more valued than she had in long time.

"Thank you," Luciana said, smiling at him. "I hope you feel the same when the project is done."

"If what I see here is any indication, I'm sure I will."

They regarded each other briefly. He had bright blue eyes that seemed to take her in, and, despite the close scrutiny, Luciana didn't feel intimidated but respected. She guessed him to be in his mid-thirties, and her curiosity of earlier piqued, several questions rushing to her mind. When her eyes slid to his left hand, she held the tablet with both her hands to keep her fingers occupied.

No ring.

As she looked back at him, the corner of his mouth rose. He'd caught her checking his ring finger.

Luciana's cheeks heated, and she rushed for something to say. "So how did you come to be a museum owner?"

His expression softened. "I guess you could say it runs in the family." He started walking toward the lobby, and Luciana adjusted her pace to his.

A bronze bust on a marble pedestal sat to the side of the staircase and Matt paused beside it. "This is Thomas Garrison, my great-great-great-grandfather. He came from England and settled Hudson Springs in 1829, hiring Irish and Italian immigrants to work in his textile factory."

Luciana touched the metal. "He looks fierce."

"History accounts would agree with you. Even though he brought growth to the area, he didn't always have the best interest of his employees in mind. Most of the Garrisons that came after him kind of followed in his footsteps, and that created a rift between the locals."

"Let me guess. Garrisons on one side and Kerrisons on the other?"

He let out a low chuckle. "With other families following each group."

"What happened to the factory?"

"The original one burned down in a mystery fire in the late nineteen thirties." He stepped to the wall on the right side where a large painting hung, depicting a building that reminded her of the dark, imposing structures from the Industrial Revolution era in England.

"Impressive," she said.

He gestured to another frame, this one holding a black and white photograph. "A new, bigger factory was halfway through construction at the other end of town, which closed for operations in 1978. By that time, my grandfather, Cornelius Garrison the third, had diversified his financial interests into other areas and the closing didn't set him back."

"That's quite the legacy you have," she said.

Matt winced lightly. "You could say that. There's a lot of animosity toward the history of this town and I'm trying to honor the past." He tilted his head and gestured to the room at large. "This building was a private residence for a long time. Given its central location and architectural features, I always thought it would make the perfect museum."

He cocked his head to one side, as if deep in thought and lost for a moment in whatever skeletons his family had.

"And here you are," Luciana said.

He straightened and smiled. "And here I am, trying to open a museum half the town doesn't want to see."

Luciana frowned, but before she had the chance to ask a question, he went on. "Textiles are part of the history in this area, even if they're not politically correct, and I'm hoping the exhibit will change the public opinion and bridge the gap of understanding."

They walked back to the workroom, and he stopped in front of the table where the binder lay open. "It's very exciting to finally see these pieces get the spot they deserve." He glanced at the clock on the wall. "I took enough of your time already. This is what happens when someone asks me how I became the museum owner. I'm sorry."

He smiled again and Luciana found herself responding in kind. "No need to apologize. I find textiles fascinating, as you can probably guess."

"I'm in town until after Christmas, and I'd like to return to see the progress of the restoration before I leave." He extended his arm, and his large hand gripped hers firmly yet gently.

She smiled at him. "Anytime you want."

As he left the workroom, Matt paused at the door and looked back at her and smiled, then turned toward the front of the building.

He had quite the smile, and he seemed to know he did.

Luciana walked back to her desk, thinking about the encounter. What was it with all the intriguing men in this town?

CHAPTER FIVE

Thursday morning arrived too early for Luciana. Although by now the jet lag should have been on the downswing, she would have liked to stay in bed a little longer. Her second-floor room at the River View Inn faced downtown, and the Christmas lights were still on in the early morning grayness. She pulled a blanket off the bed and settled on the window seat.

On the east side, a peculiar scene took place. A large group of people followed a couple walking leisurely down the street. After noting the video cameras, reflectors, dimmers, and sound equipment, she surmised they must be the camera crew from the wedding channel Mrs. Wells had been talking about almost every day since Luciana's arrival. She watched them for a few minutes, and when the town's Christmas lights turned off, they paused the filming and congregated in small groups before they started packing up.

How fun to be in town when a documentary was being filmed. She'd have to find out the title and try to watch it when it became available.

Pulling away from the window, she stood and laid the blanket back down on the bed. When she reached for her phone on the bedside table, it was turned off, and it hadn't charged during the night. She plugged it, and the notifications pinged. There was a text from an unknown number, and her heart flipped.

Hi. This is Jack DiLorenzo. Is this Luciana?

He'd sent it after dinner and she'd missed it.

She sat on the edge of the bed to send a reply. **Yes, it's Luciana. Sorry. I didn't see this until now.**

What if he thought she'd ignored him on purpose? A new text popped up.

No problem. Just wanted to make sure I sent it to the right number.

I get off at six tomorrow. Does the invitation still stand? She texted back.

Yes, of course, came his prompt reply. **I can pick you up at the inn.**

That would be great. 6:15?

I'll be there.

Are you always up this early? Luciana replied, not ready to say goodbye yet.

Baker's hours. And you?

Jet lag.

Your reason is more glamorous than mine, came Jack's reply.

She smiled. **Yours sounds more delicious.**

You'll have to come by to see for yourself.

I'll come for lunch.

I'll look forward to it.

Me too. She grinned, unable to hold it back.

Was she flirting with Jack DiLorenzo? It had been so long, she wasn't quite sure what she was doing. Whatever it was, her heart felt light and happy, and she was still smiling.

Her chest squeezed with a twinge of longing. When was the last time she'd wanted to befriend a man? Her life was divided between work and family, and she couldn't remember the last time she'd gone on a date. Something drew her closer to Jack, and she didn't understand the reason behind the feeling. With only two weeks in town, expecting more out of a short work trip was unrealistic. Wasn't it?

With a sigh, she put the phone down and stood. Might as well get ready for the day.

Her morning at the museum was fast paced, despite her earlier than normal arrival. By now, half the collection had been cleaned and repaired, and the restoration was progressing on schedule. Luciana had cataloged those pieces and put some preliminary touches in the presentation of the collection. As it usually happened with most of her projects abroad, she wouldn't be in Hudson Springs when the exhibit was set to open, but she was committed to do as much for it as she could before she left.

The finger lace veil took most of her time. She supervised Oliver with the simpler knit pieces, but the veil was her project, as it required more expertise and attention to detail than the rest of the collection. The yarn was spun very thinly, and the lace knitting was delicate and a true work of art. She didn't want to make a mistake. In her notebook, she sketched the pattern and measurements, as she often did with favorite pieces. It was incremental work, as each step of the process called for a pause before the next one could be completed, allowing her to multi-task with other pieces and coordinate with Oliver.

While the veil waited for the next step, Luciana separated the baby items. She worked in silence at one of the tables by the large window, with all the pieces laid out in front of her. The pale, winter sunlight filtered through the glass and warmed her fingers as she repaired, darned, and stitched. She relished her time with these articles of clothing, with the soft colors and natural textures, and often thought about the people who had knitted them and for whom they had been knit. Had the knitter been a mother or a grandmother? How many babies had worn each piece? What about the wedding veil? Had the bride knitted it herself? How old had she been when she got married? Life had been so different back then, so much harder. Preserving the history was an important part of the work, even when the provenance was unknown, as it often happened. These knitted garments had been important to someone's life, and as Luciana spared her thoughts to them, they became an intrinsic part of her.

The baby pieces gave her the inspiration for the gift she was knitting for Carlota, her cousin's baby and her goddaughter. While she worked on the restoration, her fingers knew what to do, movement after movement. It left her with free time to think about her early morning exchange with Jack.

Almost too much time to think.

Oliver poked a head in from the other room. "I'm heading out to lunch."

Luciana glanced at the wall on the clock. "I'll be going soon too." She picked up another item and matched it to the swatch samples in the binder. "I just have a few more pieces to sort through."

She looked forward to going to the café. Usually, when she traveled to a new city, whether in Portugal or abroad, she tried new restaurants and out-the-way eateries almost every day. It was one way she had to immerse herself in the local culture. For being a small town, Hudson Springs had enough variety, but she didn't feel inclined to try other places. As good as the food was at the DiLorenzo's, there was something more enticing. Or someone.

Luciana stopped the direction of her thoughts and questioned herself. Did she have the right to seek a friendship with a man when she was leaving in just a few days? What could come of it? An online friendship through Facebook? If she were honest with herself, she didn't want another virtual friend; she wanted one she could go out with, even if he'd been pushed to do it by his family. The attraction was there, but it was not enough to make up for the distance that would separate her from Jack in two weeks' time.

A soft knock came at the door.

Luciana kept her eyes on the yarn samples, trying to match the best ones. "Come in."

"Augustus Wynthrop said it was okay to come back here," a male voice said, a hint of hesitation trailing the words.

Luciana looked up from the work table. "Jack?"

He entered the room with a large paper sack in his hands. "Oliver Kerrison came to the café, and when I asked him about you, he said you were still working when he'd left."

She glanced at the wall clock—less than fifteen minutes of the lunch hour were left. Luciana touched the middle of her forehead and closed her eyes. "I totally spaced it out."

"When you didn't show up for lunch, I figured you were stuck here working," Jack said with a small smile, then raised the paper sack.

Luciana left her workstation and met him at the front of the room. "You brought me lunch?"

"I didn't want you to miss your meal." He handed her the bag.

Luciana peeked inside, where she found a wrapped sandwich, a pastry, and a bottle of her favorite organic lemonade. "You brought me lunch," she repeated.

She looked up at him and he shrugged, cocking his head with a small smile. "Maybe the lunch was just an excuse."

An excuse to see her? Was that what he meant?

She looked in the bag again. "There's no receipt. How much do I owe you?"

"Nothing. It's on me."

Luciana leaned in and brushed a kiss on his face. "Thank you. That was really nice of you."

His eyes went wide. "Well, with that kind of thanks ..." He trailed off, chuckling lightly.

The air-kiss. Her cheeks heated, and she swallowed. "I'm so sorry. I totally forgot Americans don't do that here."

Jack didn't say anything, the smile still on his face. After a moment, he shifted his weight and took a step back. She realized she was too close—almost encroaching on his space. Her neck heated again and she turned to place the bag on a nearby table, trying to hide her embarrassment. What was wrong with her? She didn't usually mix up customs, or kiss unsuspecting men on the cheek. But then, when was the last time a man had brought her lunch?

"I can't eat here." She motioned to the side door. "Do you want to come with me in the staff room? Or do you have to go back?"

"I've got a few minutes," Jack said.

Luciana carried her sack, and he followed her down the corridor to the back of the building.

The room was empty when they arrived. Luciana turned on the lights and took the closest table.

"Nice room," Jack said as he looked around. After a moment, he sat on the chair opposite hers.

"I think it's a converted butler's pantry with some extra space added to it." The built-in cabinets were originals, and an apartment-size refrigerator had been tucked to the side, along with a microwave sitting on the counter next to it. The rest of the room kept most of its original charm. "So much craftsmanship in these cabinets."

"The Garrisons have always prided themselves in having the best."

Luciana raised an eyebrow. "This building belongs to the Garrisons?"

"I think one of the old Garrisons had it built as a home for his new bride. Or so legend says."

Matt Garrison hadn't mentioned anything specific. She'd have to ask him next time. "The woodwork is fantastic."

Jack looked at her. "You like old things." It was more an observation than a question.

"Old things have character and history, and history is what gives us identity."

He seemed to consider her statement, then nodded slowly.

Luciana unwrapped the sandwich. At the sight of fresh tomato, basil, and mozzarella on toasted focaccia bread, she sighed. "A caprese sandwich." She took a bite and closed her eyes at the explosion of flavor in her mouth. "The vinaigrette is perfect. And the fresh basil. Where did you get it?"

The corner of Jack's mouth upturned in a small smile. "We keep a few pots of fresh herbs inside during the winter. In the summer, we have a full herb garden." He leaned against the back of his chair, his shoulders relaxing.

His posture became more comfortable, as if they were old friends and often shared meals. Even if she was the only one eating at the moment.

Luciana kept eating. "This is an awesome sandwich. Thank you." She almost made a sound in appreciation. "How did you get started in the culinary arts? Were you one of those kids experimenting in the kitchen, or did it come later for you?"

"Growing up in a family of cooks, I learned my way around the kitchen early on. Can't say I had plans to be the café's baker."

"What did you do after high school then?"

"I went to college in California and got a degree in accounting." His tone was natural, almost matter-of-fact.

She paused to look at him. "You're an accountant?"

"I keep my license up to date, and I'm in charge of the financials for the family business. Sometimes I help friends at tax time."

"How did you end up as the baker then?"

A shadow flashed through Jack's eyes. "When my dad passed away, I came home to help Mom and Nonna."

"I'm so sorry," Luciana replied immediately. She covered his hand and gave it a squeeze, letting her fingers linger a moment longer on his.

She'd been wondering if his father did something else since she hadn't seen him at the café. "That must have been hard."

He shrugged. "It's been a while."

Despite his neutral tone, a grieved emotion darkened his eyes again. Maybe the pain wasn't fresh, but it was still there.

She held his gaze, feeling an urgency to know more about him, but sensing he wasn't quite ready.

Just then, Oliver knocked on the open door. "Sorry to interrupt. I have a question about one of the items, Luciana."

Jack stood. "I should be going."

"I'll be right there, Oliver," Luciana said, pulling away from the table.

Oliver held a thumbs-up sign and turned back the way he'd come.

Luciana threw away the garbage and kept the pastry for later, then walked beside Jack as they made their way to the workroom.

"I can't thank you enough for bringing me lunch." She added a smile to her words, hoping it was enough to tell him how much she had really appreciated it.

"You're welcome. I'm glad we had a few minutes to talk." His half-smile made an appearance again.

Although she didn't know Jack well yet, somehow she knew he was genuine, both with his time and his words.

The gentle way he looked at her warmed her heart. "I am too," she said.

For a moment, they watched each other, standing in the corridor by the open door to the workroom. Luciana moved to Jack's left just as he took a step forward, and the awkward near miss had them retreating quickly.

From the way she felt so flushed, her face must be scarlet. She tried again, resting a hand on his arm, and Jack met her halfway to steady her elbow.

She leaned the rest of the way in and brushed a kiss on his cheek. "Thanks again, Jack," she said in his ear. He smelled divine, a mix of cinnamon and spice and an all-male scent. The urge to inhale deeply rose in her chest and Luciana took a step back before she gave in to it.

Jack squeezed her arm before letting go, then walked toward the main door, his eyes soft and smiling and still locked on her. "Have a good afternoon."

Luciana raised her hand in a small wave. "You too."

How was she going to focus on all the work she had to do after his surprise visit?

FRIDAY, DECEMBER 15TH

Jack's phone rattled on the counter behind him. He removed his food-service glove and swiped at the screen.

I set up an alarm so I don't forget to break for lunch.

A grin formed on his lips as he read the text from Luciana. **Sounds like a good idea.**

Count on me for lunch. Will you be at the café or the festival?

I have to deliver cookies in the morning. I'll be at the café around noon. He'd have to go back to the festival in the afternoon to cover a shift at the booth before his tour with Luciana in the evening.

I'll be there then. This time for real.

I can deliver lunch to you again. That idea sounded better. They'd have alone time like yesterday.

That's a very sweet offer, but no. I'm already taking some of your time this evening. I promise, I'll be there.

I'll see you later then.

She sent a thumbs-up emoji, and Jack put the phone down. After washing his hands, he retrieved a new pair of gloves and put them on, then returned to the dough. The grin persisted on his face as he worked on finishing the cookies needed at the festival today.

Through the morning, every time the bell on the front door jangled, Jack poked his head from the kitchen in its direction, hoping to see the familiar red coat.

Not Luciana yet. It was too early for lunch anyway.

Jack resumed his position by the trays and cellophane wrap as he packed the cookies he'd finished in the early morning, which he'd be dropping off at the booth shortly. Although he'd be spending time with Luciana tonight at the festival, he was looking forward to meeting her at lunch.

Seeing her once a day wasn't enough.

The thought startled him. He'd only met her on Monday. Four days ago.

Jack frowned. Was he doing it again? Falling head first into a new friendship with a woman he hadn't known long?

But this was different, wasn't it? Luciana wasn't Madison, for starters. And he'd learned his lesson. No, he definitely wouldn't be making the same mistake.

When Jack arrived at the festival, his cousins greeted him anxiously.

"About time," said Peter, one of his cousins from the Barisone family, on his mother's side.

Jack opened the back of the van and picked up a stack of trays. "How many do you have left?"

"We're down to one tray of the *pignoli*."

The traditional Italian cookies were the most popular item they sold during the season. "Not anymore," Jack replied as he placed the trays behind the booth's counter.

"Can you stay for a bit?" Peter asked.

Jack checked the time on his phone. "I can. As long as I'm back at the café by noon."

The lines were steady with a few breaks here and there. Jack helped with the hot chocolate while his cousins sold cookies and pizelli, and they chatted easily with the festival goers, many of them guests who'd come to ski at the resort. Later, when the lights turned on after dark, whole families would come and the area in the town square would fill to capacity. Jack would be there with Luciana.

Maybe he was looking forward to it more than

he'd anticipated.

Jack left the booth with a promise to return later, and started his way back toward the truck. A flash of red caught his attention. Ahead of him, a woman in a red coat walked beside a tall man in a dark wool coat.

Was that Luciana? And who was the guy with her?

His muscles tensed as realization settled in. From the cut and color of the coat and the brown hair, he was positive it was indeed Luciana. He wasn't sure about the man, but it looked to be Matt Garrison.

Jack's shoulders sagged, and he slipped into the front of the truck, then took a side street that would lead him to the café ahead of them. Sometimes he parked out front, but not today.

When he entered through the service door, Jack hung his coat and checked his phone. No messages. He'd half-expected to see one from Luciana canceling their outing tonight. But there was nothing, and he took that to mean their plans were still on. At least, until further notice.

He washed his hands and donned his apron, his thoughts whirling with different scenarios and possibilities he hadn't entertained before. He didn't have any right to assume anything about Luciana. She could make her own choices. Just because Jack thought they'd made a sort of connection didn't mean she'd felt it too.

Besides, next to Matt Garrison, Jack didn't measure up. He was painfully aware of that.

By now, Luciana and Matt Garrison had probably

entered the café already. Jack had planned to meet her to take her order, but that was too much to deal with.

His phone vibrated, and a text from Luciana filled the screen.

I'm here. At the table by the front.

Of course she was.

As Jack contemplated what to do, Mom peeked in the kitchen. "Luciana is asking about you. Did you tell her you'd be here?"

"I did." He palmed his phone in his front pocket and squared his shoulders, putting on a pleasant expression.

When he entered the café's floor, his eyes scanned the floor and stopped at the table Luciana usually took. A group of young skiers sat there, and the tightening between Jack's shoulder blades immediately eased out. He'd come to think of that table as Luciana's spot, and the prospect of seeing her there with a man had not been a welcome one.

Mom walked in the other direction, and he followed her to a table at the opposite corner where Luciana sat across from Matt Garrison.

That burning sensation pricked Jack in the chest.

Luciana turned to look at him and her expression bloomed into a radiant smile. "Hi, Jack."

That smile. Was she really that happy to see him? Jack smiled back, momentarily forgetting she wasn't alone. "Hi, Luciana. Glad you made it." He was glad she'd come, even if she wasn't alone. He looked at

Matt Garrison and nodded. "Matt."

Matt smiled and returned the greeting, quickly refocusing his attention on Luciana.

As much as Jack would like to find fault with Matt Garrison, he was the kind of man who treated everyone well. If Luciana chose to go with Matt instead of him, Jack wouldn't like it, but at least she would be in good hands.

Jack took their order and walked back to the kitchen, swallowing the bitter tang in his mouth. Matt Garrison was interested in Luciana. He hadn't flirted with her, not in front of Jack, but his body language was clear to read, and Jack couldn't begrudge him.

As he realized his lack of gumption, Jack was more disgusted with himself than with the situation. Why couldn't he make up his mind about what he wanted? It would save a lot of emotional investment on his part.

Mom and Nonna hovered too closely, serving Luciana and Matt Garrison and going back several times to check on them. Maybe a little too often. He'd have to remind Mom and Nonna of the fine line between service and stalking.

Despite telling himself not to look in their direction, Jack did, as if a magnet pulled him toward Luciana. She and Matt looked at ease, and Jack couldn't help but wonder what they were talking about.

Forty minutes later, Luciana stood at the entrance to the kitchen.

"Your mom said it was okay if I came to say

goodbye," Luciana said.

Jack wiped his hands on a hand towel and approached her. "Of course." He smiled, hoping it looked more natural than he felt.

"We're going back to the museum now." She looked over her shoulder to where Matt stood a few feet away. He raised a hand and Jack waved back. "Mr. Wynthrop is closing earlier today. I'll be done at five. We could go earlier to the festival, if you're free."

The expectation in her eyes threw him off for a second. Luciana wasn't canceling their tour to the festival; she was asking to leave earlier.

"I'm free." He didn't need to sleep an extra hour. "Pick you up at five fifteen?"

"That would be great," she said with a smile.

Maybe it really would be great. Even though Mom and Nonna had contrived for him to take Luciana to the festival, he was looking forward to it.

CHAPTER SIX

When Jack entered the foyer of the River View Inn, Luciana was coming down the main staircase.

She smiled when she saw him, and his heart stuttered. He'd been thinking about the cheek kiss, the barely-there contact of her lips and face touching his, the way her breath had fanned his skin. Only Mom and Nonna ever kissed his cheeks, and it was not the same.

So not the same.

"Perfect timing," Luciana said when she reached the landing.

She wore a hand knit cap, and her chocolate-brown hair touched her shoulders. He'd only seen her with a ponytail before and liked the look of her hair down. "Are you ready?"

"Ready as I can be." She held her hands up. "Gloves, scarf, cap, and lots of layers under my coat."

He held the front door for her. "Great. The festival is a lot of fun, but it gets cold after a little while."

Once on the sidewalk, Luciana settled beside Jack, and he adjusted his pace to hers.

"I'm glad you suggested we meet earlier," Jack said. "We'll be able to see something I'd forgotten about."

"And what's that?"

"It's a surprise. We're almost there," he said.

"A little hint? I'm dying of curiosity."

"It'll be worth it. I promise." Jack glanced at her and smiled.

He'd almost forgotten how magical it was to watch the tree lighting ceremony in person, and he wanted to see Luciana's reaction.

As they emerged into the town square, the streets were congested with families and festival goers in all directions.

Luciana stopped beside him. "You didn't tell me the whole town of Hudson Springs would be here."

Jack chuckled. "More than our town. We get visitors too."

"Yeah, tons of them."

A group of teenagers ran by and jostled Luciana toward Jack, and she hung on to his elbow to steady herself.

He reached down and grabbed her gloved hand. "What do you say we stick together? I know you can find your way back to the inn, but I'd rather not lose you in the crowd."

Luciana stepped closer. "Good plan."

They slowed and looked at each other briefly. Even with the gloves on, the warmth of Luciana's hand and the weight of her fingers wrapped in his sent a zing he hadn't expected.

Jack cut a path through the crowd with Luciana tucked in at his side until they reached the edge of the town square in front of the gazebo. At the opposite corner, directly in front of them, the Christmas tree was still unlit.

"We got here just in time," he said to Luciana. "Look on ahead now."

When the church bell struck the half hour, the thousands of lights on the twenty-two foot tree turned on.

Jack kept his eyes on Luciana, and her expression glowed at the scene before them, eyes wide and a smile illuminating her face. She said something he didn't understand, but it wasn't hard to guess how she felt about it.

"I'm so glad we came earlier," Luciana said after a few minutes. "It's been awhile since I've watched a tree lighting in person." The wonder in her tone made the sleep he lost worthwhile.

He gave her a few minutes more to enjoy it, and when the crowd started dispersing, Jack turned to her. "Let's hit the food booths first. I'm ready to show you the best of the Hudson Springs Christmas Festival."

Luciana tipped up her nose. "Show me to the roasted chestnuts. I can smell them."

Jack chuckled and tugged her hand in the right direction.

As he'd hoped, experiencing the festival with someone who'd never been there before was exactly what he needed to distract him from his old memories. He'd always liked Christmas and all the festivities around it, but it had been hard to get past his depression after Madison dumped him on Christmas Day two years ago.

With Luciana at his side, he only had to worry about an evening out with an attractive woman. No expectations and no commitments.

They walked around, and after sampling a little bit of everything, Jack steered them to the last food booth. "Let's go. I saved the best for last."

"What's this booth?" Luciana asked.

"Italian cookies and hot chocolate," he said with a smile. He swung behind the counter and pulled out a tall cup from the stack.

"Hey, Jack. Are you staying?" Ashley said, while arranging a batch of cookies on a tray.

"Luciana, this is my cousin's daughter, Ashley. And that's her dad, my cousin Peter." Peter raised a hand from the other end of the counter, where he was helping customers. "Luciana is working at the museum for two weeks."

Luciana smiled and waved at the cousins. "Hi, how are you?"

"So you're not staying to help?" Ashley asked.

"My shift's tomorrow." He grabbed a paper bag and filled it halfway with an assortment of cookies. "Today I'm showing Luciana around the Hudson Springs Christmas Festival."

Ashley glanced at Luciana. "You better hurry up with the showing," she said in a low tone. "She looks cold."

Jack called Luciana over and handed her a cup, then took a cup for himself and the paper bag.

With their palms wrapped around the steaming cups of cocoa, they could no longer hold hands and Jack missed the contact.

Luciana took a careful sip as she waited for him to come from behind the counter.

"What do you think?" he asked her.

She closed her eyes and inhaled. "I think you've been holding out on me. This is so delicious."

Jack chuckled. "It tastes better when you've been standing out in the cold." He handed her the bag of cookies. "Try one of these now."

Luciana reached in the bag and drew out a tortelli, then took a bite. "This is fantastic. What is it?"

"They're chestnut tortelli with a filling of spiced rum, chestnuts, and chocolate." Jack watched her delight.

"I'm sure people tell you all the time, but you guys must have the best baker in town."

Jack made a small bow. "Why, thank you. We like to think so, but it's not polite to brag." He chuckled lightly.

Luciana stopped. "Wait. You're the baker? I already know you make the best coffee in town, not to mention the most delicious sandwiches. And I thought you said you were the accountant."

Jack shrugged. "Accountant, barista, baker, busboy. A little of everything."

"You're a veritable Jack-of-all-trades. No pun intended." She grinned at her little joke, her eyes crinkling with joy, her cheeks rosy.

"Like I haven't heard that one before," he said with a grin of his own.

They finished their food near a free-standing gas warmer, and, as they started toward the craft and holiday decoration booths, Luciana adjusted her scarf. "I see I'll have to come back with a bag and a plan." She hopped from one foot to the other, her shoulders hunched despite her cheery expression.

She was cold. She wore a handknit scarf, hat, and gloves, but he didn't know what she was wearing under her coat. And her shoes didn't look to be warm enough. He'd been so distracted spending time with Luciana that he'd failed to remember she was probably not used to the cold weather in Hudson Springs.

He took both her hands in his and rubbed them between his. "You're freezing."

She shrugged, her smile still on. "Maybe a little."

He held on to her hand. "Come on, I have one last spot."

She gripped his hand tighter, and, as he led Luciana out of the festival grounds, he had one question burning to be asked. "You can tell me to mind my own business, but I have to ask."

Luciana slowed down and turned to him. "Ask away."

"You and Matt Garrison." He looked to her. "Is there anything—"

"Jack," a woman's voice interrupted him.

Jack went still, and Luciana came to a stop behind him, her hand letting go of his.

He wasn't prepared for this. Of all the people in town, why did he have to bump into Mrs. Parker? Hadn't the Parkers moved away right after the whole fiasco? But it was Christmas. Of course they'd return for the festival.

"Hello, Jack," Mrs. Parker said. "You're looking good."

"Mrs. Parker," he replied gravely. Too gravely. He cleared his throat. "How are you?"

"Good, good. We're in town for the festival. Can't miss that, of course."

Of course they wouldn't. Like everyone else in Hudson Springs, the family tradition was too ingrained.

The tension was palpable, and Jack didn't know what to say to disperse it. Beside him, Luciana took a step closer. For a moment, he'd forgotten she was there. When her gloved fingers found his, he grabbed on to her hand, grateful for the contact, for the support she offered.

Mrs. Parker didn't miss the gesture, and she pinned a gaze on Luciana, then turned to him. "Is this—"

"I'm Luciana," Luciana interrupted in a cheerful voice. "Don't you love this festival? I didn't expect it to be this large." She pressed closer to his side, her other hand resting on his forearm. "I'm so glad Jack is showing me around."

Her sweet smile implied a lot more than the recent friendship they had, and Jack took it unashamedly, making a show of lacing their gloved fingers, indebted to her for the quick thinking and intervention.

After another long moment, he'd had enough. "Well, I better take Luciana for some hot chocolate. If you'll excuse us."

Mrs. Parker stepped aside. "Yes, of course. Nice seeing you, Jack."

He nodded, not knowing what to say to that. There was nothing nice about the encounter—just a whole lot of awkward.

Luciana took her farthest hand away from his arm, and they walked on, still holding hands at their sides.

"You are a very perceptive woman, Luciana," he said at last. He relaxed his hand, but she didn't let go, and the relief passed through him in a long exhale.

"It looked like you needed a good friend," she said simply.

She had no idea.

He found the first shortcut toward home and steered them that way.

"It's my turn to say 'you can tell me to mind my own business', but who was that?" Luciana asked.

"My fiancée's mother," he replied.

Jack had a fiancée?

The questions simmered as Luciana followed Jack past a driveway and a dead garden. They'd walked a block away from the town square and the festival, maybe even less, but she didn't recognize the area.

He hadn't said a word since meeting the woman on the sidewalk in what must have been the most awkward encounter Luciana had witnessed. Her chest still pricked at the revelation of his words, but she held her judgment back until Jack gave her an explanation.

"How does a fireplace sound?" He pulled a set of keys from his pocket. "And maybe a warm dinner?"

"Are you serious?" Her mood picked up. As fun as the festival was, her feet were frozen to the bone, and she was ready for some warmth. She was ready for answers too.

He led her into a front room, and she relaxed. The indoor temperature wrapped around her like warm flannel sheets, as the ones she had in her bed in Lisbon.

"Is this your home?" she asked.

Jack turned on the lights then moved to a dormant fireplace. With the turn of a switch, the flames flicked to life.

"I live with my Mom and Nonna. My grandmother," he corrected. He motioned her over. "Come sit by the fire. I'll be right back." He turned the closest stuffed chair to face the gas flames, then took her coat and hung it in the closet.

Luciana approached the chair and removed her hat, scarf, and gloves, placing them on the coffee table. She sat down, extending her feet and hands toward the heat. She looked around the room.

The fireplace sat between two windows, with a grouping of chairs around it. Next to it, a floor-to-ceiling Christmas tree, laden with ornaments and lights, dominated the room with its quiet presence. On the wall behind her, a set of shelves displayed a few books and several family photos in small frames. Luciana stood, intent on taking a closer look, but just then Jack's mother entered the room.

"First he freezes you, then he forgets you," she said as she approached Luciana with a pair of slippers in her hands. "Here, put these on."

"Mrs. DiLorenzo, hi." Luciana stood and held the slippers. "I don't want to intrude—"

"Nonsense," she waved her hand. "You need a chance to warm up. Just follow me to the back."

Luciana edged to the side and quickly replaced her shoes with the lined slippers, then walked behind Jack's mom through a dining room and a short hallway, emerging into a spacious kitchen, where Jack stood at the stove.

"Jack, you forgot Luciana in the front room," his mother said.

Jack turned and smiled. "I knew you'd get her, so technically I didn't forget." He mouthed *sorry* to Luciana, and she smiled at him.

He was back to being the carefree Jack, and the tension from meeting the woman was gone from his expression and posture. Luciana could wait for the chance to ask her questions.

The kitchen was wide, and it opened to a family room where another gas fireplace crackled happily. Already Luciana's feet had warmed up, and her heart didn't stand a chance at the sight of Jack with his sleeves rolled up to his elbows.

"Ah, *Luchana*, you join us," Jack's grandmother said. She raised a knitting needle in greeting, sitting in the family room.

Luciana approached, curious to see the project the older lady was working on. "What are you knitting?"

"Hats for the little ones," she replied.

"Come, sit." Paola guided Luciana to the island and a bar-height chair.

"I'll have this ready in five minutes," Jack said, as he stirred and added ingredients to a sauté pan.

"How's the project coming, Luciana?" Paola asked. "Tell us what you're working on."

"I'm working at the museum to help restore a collection of nineteenth century knitted garments." Luciana spent a few minutes explaining the scope of her work to Jack's mother and grandmother.

"For how long?" Nonna asked.

"I'm leaving on December twenty-seventh in the evening." She had a red-eye flight to Lisbon.

"You are missing Christmas with your boyfriend?" Nonna asked, her eyes still on the hat she knit.

Luciana smiled. "No boyfriend. Just my family and extended family."

"Do you have a close family?" Jack asked over his shoulder.

She nodded. "I think we are close. I have three brothers, one older and two younger, and we try to get together as often as we can." With everyone so busy, sometimes it went a few months before they had the chance to meet. She was glad she'd seen Filipe when she'd visited with Catarina in Sete Fontes.

Jack turned off the burner and pulled a plate from the cabinet. "I have three sisters, one older and two younger."

He met Luciana's eyes, and she smiled at him, unable to pull her gaze away. She wanted to believe there was a simple explanation to what had happened at the festival, but knew instinctively he wouldn't talk until his mother and grandmother had left.

Jack scooped drained spaghetti onto a plate, piling it into a swirl. From the other pan, he dished a portion of the homemade tomato sauce he'd been working on, and then he grated Parmesan from a small block. He finished with a pinch of chopped herbs.

"Hope you like Italian," he said, setting the plate in front of Luciana.

Paola added a set of utensils, a napkin, and a glass of water. "We also have red wine, juice, and sodas. What would you like to drink?"

"Water is fine. Thank you. This looks fantastic." Luciana held her fork. "Am I the only one eating?"

"We already ate," said Paola. "In fact, it's time to help Nonna with her medicine before bed time. We need a good night's rest. Tomorrow's the Santa Parade, and we can't miss that." She touched Luciana on the shoulder. "Luciana, it was great seeing you. We hope you'll come again before you leave."

Jack came around the counter and kissed his mom's cheek, then walked over to his grandma and did the same. "Have a good night, you two."

Nonna patted his face. "Be good, *ragazzo*."

"Always, Nonna," he replied with a boyish expression.

They watched as the ladies left the room. "They remind me of my mom and grandma," Luciana said to Jack.

"Is this the same grandma who wants you to go wedding dress shopping?" Jack asked.

Luciana nodded with a chuckle. "Yes, my grandmother from the Romano side. She only has sons, but she's close to my mother and my aunts." Despite her meddling, Avó Teresa meant well, and Luciana loved her.

Jack got a plate and joined Luciana at the island.

After a few bites of the dinner Jack had cooked for her, she was in heaven. "This sauce tastes like homegrown summer tomatoes. How did you do it? Do you have a greenhouse tucked in the back?"

"No, but we do grow our own tomatoes and other vegetables. I cook the sauce when the tomatoes are ripe, and Mom and Nonna can it in jars while it's fresh." He gestured to an empty glass jar sitting by the stove. "All I had to do was boil the spaghetti and warm the sauce."

"Are you a chef too? This plate looks amazing, and the sauce is divine. I'd pay good money for a jar of it."

Jack stood and walked to a pantry in the corner of the kitchen. He returned a few minutes later with two jars and set them in front of her. "This one is traditional and the other is *puttanesca*, with kalamata olives and capers."

Luciana stared at the jars. "I can't take these. They'll break."

"I'll give you a couple of zipper plastic bags to put them in. Just pack them in the middle of the suitcase among your clothes. They'll be just fine."

"Okay, I'll do it. If I end up with tomato sauce in my sweaters, I'll blame it on you." She took the last bite, savoring the rich flavors.

For dessert, Jack served her a big, fat slice of the richest, most decadent tiramisu she'd ever had, and Luciana ate in silence, wondering how this man with such a talent for baking and cooking delicious food was still single.

Then she remembered the encounter at the festival. Maybe he wasn't married, but he had a fiancée. Or did he?

She shifted in her seat and put down the fork. When she met Jack's eyes, his expression had the same kind of guarded curiosity she felt at the moment.

A prick of doubt flashed through her. Did she really want to get past the privacy of friendly acquaintance?

He studied her, and the vulnerability she saw in his eyes lent her the courage to want to put her heart on the line without the fear of rejection. She hadn't come on this trip looking for a relationship. In fact, the opposite was true.

But here she was, wishing the promise of something beyond friendship could be as real as the man sitting across from her. And if it was wrong to feel this way after having met him four days ago, then she didn't want to know about it.

Jack cleared his throat. "You're probably wondering about that woman we met." His brown eyes pulled her in, warm and tentative. Did he feel like her, wanting to confide but holding back for fear of rejection?

Luciana nodded. "The mother of your fiancée? It crossed my mind." She relaxed against the high-back chair. "And, for the record, the thing Matt Garrison and I have is nothing but professional." Matt had dropped by the museum to talk to Mr. Wynthrop, and when he'd invited her for lunch, she'd accepted. Going to DiLorenzo's had been his suggestion, and she'd agreed with it since she was already going there to eat.

Jack's shoulders relaxed. "I didn't have the right to ask."

"Curiosity doesn't bother me, especially when I'm curious too."

Jack nodded. "Mrs. Parker is Madison's mom, and Madison was my fiancée." His eyes shifted, and he swallowed. "She—we broke up almost two years ago around this time of year."

"I'm sorry." She leaned forward and touched his hand. "No wonder it was so awkward."

Jack chuckled. "Yes, it was. The last time I saw Madison's mom, I was still engaged to her daughter."

"It probably didn't help that I stood right next to you."

He turned her hand in his and gave it a squeeze. "It helped me a lot, to have you by my side like that. Thank you." A small smile lifted the corner of his mouth.

Luciana's cheeks heated under his gaze, and she shrugged, still holding on to his hand.

Jack let go. "Now I made you uncomfortable." He stood and took their plates to the sink. "Enough serious for now. I don't want to scare you off."

He winked at her, and Luciana chuckled. She appreciated his effort in making the conversation less intense.

Jack led the way back to the living room, and they sat by the fireplace.

"What are your plans for the weekend?" he asked.

Her shoes had dried, and she put them on. "Tomorrow I have some work to do at the museum. Sunday I'm free, but I haven't thought about what I want to do yet."

"The Santa Parade is tomorrow at nine in the morning, if you can make it."

"I could go in to work a little later and then stay later, if I need to." She stood and gathered her coat, scarf, gloves, and hat. "I better go. It's getting late."

Jack got his coat from the rack. "I'll drive you home."

Luciana slipped her hands in her pockets while she waited for him. "Thank you. The inn is so close, I should probably say no. But the thought of walking back in this cold..." She grimaced.

Once they arrived at the inn, Jack walked Luciana to the front door.

"Thank you for the tour and dinner and everything else."

His soft smile made an appearance. "I had a lot of fun."

"I did too," she said. It had been a surprising evening, and she had truly enjoyed his company.

She leaned in and kissed his cheek, and Jack's arms came around her for a moment. Luciana closed her eyes, taking in the warmth of his body, the weight of his hands on her arms, his masculine scent. The small hairs at the back of her neck stood on end, and heat radiated from her middle.

Jack pulled back a little and met her eyes. "Will you come for dinner tomorrow after work? I'll pick you up."

She nodded. "I will; thank you."

"And the parade? Full disclosure—Mom and Nonna will be there, and other family members. Probably lots of them."

"I don't have a problem with that. I'm more worried about you getting sick of me." She softened her words with a teasing smile.

"Not possible," Jack whispered in her ear, then brushed a kiss on her cheek.

Luciana touched the spot on her skin and smiled.

Halfway to his truck, he turned back to her. "Have you ever been skiing?"

"Never," she said with a half-amused frown.

"You just got yourself plans for Sunday. We'll talk about it tomorrow."

Luciana waved as Jack pulled away from the curb. It would take a while to fall asleep tonight.

CHAPTER SEVEN

SUNDAY, DECEMBER 17TH

$\mathcal{L}$uciana couldn't believe she and Jack were on their way to the ski resort located forty-five minutes away from Hudson Springs, to the northeast. She'd spent Saturday evening at the DiLorenzo's home for dinner, and, although she was nervous, Jack had convinced her to go skiing.

Jack picked her up after breakfast this morning and took her to his home to get ski clothes he'd borrowed for her to wear. According to him, they'd be renting the skis, boots, and poles at the resort.

She was looking forward to the trip—but more excited about spending time with Jack than the actual skiing part. She was also glad she didn't have to work on Sunday and grateful Jack had offered to drive her to see something other than Hudson Springs, as charming as the small town was.

As they made the gradual ascent toward Mount Hudson, the blanket of snow on the ground grew from a light dusting to a few solid centimeters, covering all the surfaces with a white powder that shimmered in the pallid sun.

She looked out the window, fascinated at the view. "It's so pretty."

"Have you never seen snow before?" Jack asked.

"Not in real life. The ski resort in Portugal is several hours away from Lisbon, and I haven't had the chance to travel there before."

"We might get some snowfall before you leave."

Luciana looked at Jack. "I hope it does. I'd love to see it."

On the side of the road, a large sign announced *Mount Hudson Ski Resort. Base: 1,148 ft; Summit: 2100 ft.*

"What does that mean?" Luciana asked.

Jack glanced at it. "It's the altitude at the base of the mountain and at the highest peak."

She pulled out her phone and calculated the numbers to the metric system. "Between three hundred fifty and six hundred forty meters. Not very high." Maybe skiing wouldn't be so bad after all. "The highest mountain in Portugal is just under two thousand meters."

"This one here is nothing like the mountains in Utah or Colorado, but we get enough snow for winter sports. It's a popular destination this time of year, and lots of skiers end up in town for the festival too."

"Are the skiers the ones wearing the bright jackets and paper tags on their zippers?"

"Yes, those are the skiers. The paper tags are called ski passes or lift tickets," Jack said. "The ticket gives us access to the mountain and ski areas."

Luciana glanced at the snow clothes she wore—the black pants and pink jacket, which were all insulated and waterproof—plus the layers of underthings she also had on. In addition, Jack had procured gloves and a helmet with a sun visor.

After a few minutes, a large building made of logs came into view. Other smaller buildings in the same rustic style stood to both sides, like a village, forming a striking view against the white of the snow.

"We're here," Jack said. He pulled into a parking spot, and they exited the truck.

The brightness from the sunlight bouncing on the snow surprised Luciana, and she shielded her eyes as she looked around. Families with children, groups of young people, and older people of all ages milled around in the area.

"It's a lot more crowded than I thought," she said to Jack.

"A lot of people take advantage of the weekend. Plus, school's out for winter break, and this is a resort with terrain for beginners, which makes it really popular for families."

She followed Jack to the main building where they purchased lift tickets, then went out the back door to the rental barn for boots, skis, and poles.

Much to her relief, Jack had made arrangements for a thirty-minute beginner's lesson that went over basic procedures and safety measures. Jack stood to the side while Luciana and five children of various ages listened to the instructor.

At the end of the lesson, the children scattered to their waiting families, and she watched them as they skied away confidently.

Jack approached her. "What do you think? Are you up for trying one of the short trails?"

Luciana hung on to the ski poles and concentrated on staying upright. "How did those kids manage to make it look so easy?" she said to Jack.

He chuckled. "I bet this was not their first time. The resort has special programs for school children."

At Jack's suggestion and under his nearby presence, they made their way to the ski lifts, which looked more like suspended swing chairs.

She hesitated.

"Grab your poles in your left hand and guide yourself to the seat with your right," Jack said.

Luciana nodded and followed him as they positioned themselves next in the queue. When they sat down, the chair rocked, and she grabbed the side with her free hand, gritting her teeth.

Jack pulled down the safety guard in front of them and smiled at her. "There. That wasn't so hard, was it?"

She closed her eyes and inhaled deeply. "Ask me later."

Jack touched her arm. "Are you afraid of heights?"

"I might be." Luciana looked at him, softening her expression into a tentative smile.

He frowned, worry in his face. "Why didn't you tell me? We didn't have to do this."

"I didn't know." She shrugged apologetically. "I've never been on one of these before."

"Just look straight ahead and appreciate the view," Jack said. "We're almost there."

As the chair-lift ascended along the side of the mountain, the view broadened over the trees. Luciana adjusted her goggles and took a deep breath. She focused on ignoring the sensation of floating in the air and the knowledge of the lack of net to catch her if something went wrong, relaxing instead and looking over the snow-capped trees.

The feelings came one after the other. First serenity, then peace—however brief it was. This was the kind of experience she'd take away with her, sitting above the ground next to Jack. He told her childhood experiences of skiing with his family, amusement in his voice.

When they approached the ground, Jack lifted the bar. "Get ready to exit."

He touched his feet to the ground and stood effortlessly, walking away from the chair. Luciana waited for the chair to stop before she placed her feet down on solid snow-packed dirt, then rose as she'd seen Jack do. Only the chair didn't stop. It kept going before lurching around the bend and hitting Luciana in the back of her legs.

She went face first on the ground, getting the air knocked out of her lungs. Someone yelled her name. A strong hand pulled her arm by the elbow and dragged her across the snow, filling the inside of her jacket with slush and snow. Really cold slush.

After a long minute, someone turned her over from her belly onto her back and brushed the snow off the visor.

"Luciana," Jack said. "Are you okay?"

His words sounded muffled to her ears, and she lifted her hands to grab the sides of the helmet.

"Easy there," he said.

"Did the chair hit her in the head?" A man asked.

It had happened too fast, but she was sure she'd been hit in the back on her knees. "Knees," she said. "In the knees."

Jack and the other man talked, and a moment later Jack's hands came around her neck. She became aware of someone else removing the helmet from her head, sliding it off slowly. Once free from the restricting piece of equipment, Luciana blinked and sat up.

"How are you feeling?" Jack asked. "Does anything hurt?"

"Other than my pride, you mean?" She smiled and moved to stand from the ground.

Jack caught her hand and helped her the rest of the way until she felt steady on her feet. "What happened?" he asked.

"I thought the chair would stop when I stood up and I didn't move out of the way fast enough."

"I'm sorry," Jack said. "I thought you noticed the lifts don't stop."

"Don't worry about it," she said to him. "I'm fine." The embarrassment was definitely larger than her injuries.

A man handed her helmet to Jack, and he thanked him. Luciana had hoped nobody had noticed her fall, but judging from the crowd that had started dispersing from around them, there had been plenty of witnesses to her humiliation.

Her cheeks heated, and she turned around, shaking the snow off her pants and jacket. Every time she moved, the snow melted, and she winced at the cold and wet next to her skin.

She took the helmet from Jack and put it on, then pulled the visor up and held on to the poles. "Is this the only way down?"

He nodded. "Let's take the flatter run, and you can set the pace."

Luciana placed the poles in the ground and stood in position, trying to recollect all the information she'd gained recently, and failing to remember any of it. After a long moment, she took a breath and gave herself a small push.

Jack went on ahead and showed her the easiest way, and she was passed even by young children, adding to her mortification. The back of her legs still hurt from the impact of the chair, and her undershirt was now all wet, spreading the cold to her chest. With the effort of keeping upright and following Jack,

Luciana started sweating. He stopped frequently to wait for her and encourage her to keep going, and she admired his patience with her.

By the time they arrived near the main lodge, Luciana's body was shaking from the descent and from the cold of the snow against her skin. She dropped the poles and worked on getting the boots out from the skis.

After removing his skis, Jack approached. "Here, let me help you."

She thanked him and then crossed her arms over her chest, her teeth chattering beyond her control. Luciana set her jaw firmly to stop it.

When he stood, he paused to watch her. "Are you okay? You're shaking."

She smiled tightly. "I'm wet. Snow got inside my jacket." As if the fall hadn't been enough.

Jack grabbed her skis. "Come on. Let's return the rentals so we can get you out of those wet clothes."

Twenty minutes later, Luciana sat in front of a fire in the mezzanine level of the lodge's main hall. Jack bought her a sweatshirt with the resort's logo and a plaid blanket and, after she changed, he took her to a relatively secluded corner, setting her up with a mug of hot chocolate.

Curled up in a plush chair under warm flannel, Luciana was finally warm.

"How are you feeling?" Jack asked.

"Much better. Thank you," she replied.

"Ready to hit the slopes?" he asked with a teasing smile.

Luciana chuckled. "Maybe some time, but definitely not today." She took a sip, then wrapped both her hands around the mug. "Thanks for the sweatshirt and the blanket, and for being so patient with me."

"You're welcome. Staying wet until we got home wasn't a good idea."

Other people might have not worried about her being wet. Jack was a considerate man, and he put other's needs ahead of his own without any hesitation. The emotion swelled in her chest, gratitude and appreciation for the friendship they'd formed in such a short amount of time.

What about the attraction? Was it one-sided on her part? Had she imagined the way he looked at her sometimes, the tingles that ran hot in close proximity of each other?

This wasn't what she'd come for on this trip. Finding a connection with a man was the last thing she'd expected, especially at this point in her life. The irony wasn't lost in her—she'd left Portugal to escape the wedding preparations of her Romano cousins, hoping to forget her lonely status, only to stumble into a man she hadn't planned to find.

Ironic didn't begin to cover it.

What would happen when she left after Christmas?

CHAPTER EIGHT

Luciana grabbed a pencil and twisted her hair into a messy bun. One more week before she left. With Christmas Eve on Sunday and Christmas Day on Monday, she only had five more days of work, and they would go by fast. They always did. At least all the projects were coming along on time, thanks to a meticulous schedule and Oliver's assistance.

Across the room, her phone vibrated on the desktop. She turned to the sound, hope surging inside her. Placing the sweater she was working on to the side, Luciana walked over and swiped at the screen.

Are you coming for lunch?

A text from Jack, as she'd wished.

If I cut my lunch hour in half and eat while I write my reports, I'll have more free time later, she typed.

Luciana bit her lip, hoping Jack caught her meaning.

Do you have plans for later?

Not yet, she replied.

Luciana, will you come over for dinner tonight?

I'd love too. Thank you.

Looking forward to seeing you, he said.

After Friday night, when Jack had brought her to his home for a late dinner following their time at the festival, Luciana had spent dinners with the DiLorenzos every evening. Jack's mother and grandmother had invited her for Saturday, and Jack had brought her over on Sunday after their trip to the ski resort, and the invitations kept coming this week as well. The DiLorenzo hospitality helped Luciana feel at home, distracting her from missing her family, especially as Christmas got closer.

A small smile tugged at the corner of her mouth. She couldn't help it. Spending the evening in Jack's company was definitely worth cutting her lunchtime short. Half an hour later, one of Jack's young cousins delivered a sandwich and a pastry in a paper bag. Luciana put it in the lunchroom's small refrigerator and sent Jack a message.

Thank you for lunch. I'll have you know, I was about ready to call in.

Just thought I'd save you some time, he answered.

You always think of everything.

His reply didn't come right away. She was about to put the phone down when a new message popped up.

Maybe because I'm always thinking of you.

Luciana's heart jumped when she read the words.

They'd been flirting lightly since last Friday, but not this overtly.

What could she say to him? She struggled to come up with an appropriate reply. Why was she so competent in everything except when it came to dealing with men? Was there even an emoji that said I-hear-you-but-I-don't-know-what-to-say-yet?

Before the pause got too awkward, Luciana selected the winky face and sent it. Not exactly what she wanted to say, but better than leaving his message unacknowledged. She slipped the phone in her pocket, but the distraction proved to be too great. A few minutes later, Luciana walked to the small office and placed the phone inside her purse so she could focus on her work for the rest of the afternoon.

Oliver worked beside her in the exhibit room as they placed several parts of the collection in their final spots.

"My cousin Lily would like to meet you before you leave," Oliver said.

Luciana raised an eyebrow. "About the exhibit?" Why would a local resident want to meet her?

Oliver held the sweater in place while Luciana arranged it on the male mannequin. "She's in the knitting business too. Lily owns the local yarn store," he said.

Luciana paused. "How come I didn't know there's a yarn store in Hudson Springs?" She hadn't had a lot of time to explore the town, but she had walked to and from the downtown area a few times by now.

"It's three blocks east from the town square. You probably didn't go in that direction yet."

She hadn't.

He paused before they moved to the child-size mannequin. "Can I take you by to meet Lily after work?"

Luciana smiled. "Sure, I'd love to meet your cousin. Besides, yarn stores are my weakness. How could I pass that up?" She usually made the time to visit the local yarn stores in the cities where she worked. It had become a tradition of sorts.

Twelve minutes after leaving the museum with Oliver, Luciana stopped in front of the two-story building with a covered porch. The sign read *The Knotty Knitters*. A smile rose on her lips.

She gestured toward it. "That's clever and funny," she said to Oliver.

He nodded, smiling wide. "Lily has a peculiar sense of humor."

The store had big windows decorated with a Christmas theme, and a red door with glass insets and a bell that jingled when they entered. Luciana stopped a few paces in. The indoor brick walls were filled with rows and rows of wooden cubbies containing balls and skeins of yarn in all colors and textures—a much better selection than she'd anticipated in a small town.

An old-fashioned wardrobe with its doors wide open served as a station for needles of all sizes and materials, and a nearby antique table held mismatched drawers full of accessories and notions. On the service counter—a wide wooden one full of aged patina and character—sat a vintage metal cash register, a nod to simpler times when knitting and crocheting were necessities and not just hobbies.

The Christmas decorations were all made of yarn or knitted pieces, creating an organic feel to the overall ambiance in the store.

A dark-haired woman in her late twenties approached and exchanged a brief hug with Oliver. "Oliver, I didn't know you were coming," she said.

He ducked his head. "Sorry. I didn't plan it, but I know how busy Luciana will be tomorrow and Friday, so today is the best chance." He gestured to Luciana. "This is Luciana Romano, the knit restoration specialist from Portugal. Luciana, this is my cousin Lily Kerrison, the proud owner of The Knotty Knitters."

Lily took Luciana's hand and shook it with enthusiasm. "I'm glad you came by. I read the interview *Knit International* published last year. Your work is so inspirational."

Such comments still surprised Luciana. "Thank you. I have to say, your store is just amazing. I wouldn't change a thing in here," she said sincerely.

Lily's expression relaxed into a big smile. "I think it's perfect, but I'm a little biased. Would you like me to show you around?"

Luciana followed Lily.

"I have the yarns arranged by type, color, and weight." Lily pointed at a shelf of cubbies. "Here we start with the acrylics in lace, super fine, fine, and so on."

Luciana knelt by the shelves. "I love the way you have them sorted in a rainbow pattern."

"I do it with all the yarns but especially for the acrylics which are more used by children." Lily gestured toward a corner with a sofa and a few chairs. "On Saturday mornings, I have volunteers come and teach anyone who wants to learn how to knit or crochet, and that includes a lot of kids."

"I learned to knit when I was eight years old," Luciana said, as she moved to the shelves with natural yarns.

"Me too," said Lily with a smile.

"There's been a few times when I've thought of opening a yarn store, and yours is exactly like I imagined mine to be." Luciana approached a corner where an antique desk with a hutch held spools of ribbons and an old type tray with tiny metal letters. "What is this for?"

"This is the ribbon station. There are ribbons with washing instructions, *handmade-by* or *knitted-by* ribbons, and they're all sold by the yard." She gestured at the type. "The blank ribbons are meant to be personalized."

Luciana raised an eyebrow. "Personalized with what?"

"The name of the knitter or the name of the recipient, different washing instructions, a dedicatory message—anything you can think of, I'll try to make it happen. Or I can show you how to do it too."

The corner of Luciana's mouth rose in a small smile. She could knit a piece as a gift and attach a ribbon with a message. "This is a great idea," she said to Lily.

Could Luciana find the time to knit a hat before she left? It would make the perfect gift for a new friend. "Do you have any cashmere blends?" she asked Lily.

"I actually just got something new last month," Lily said as she led Luciana to another shelf of cubbies. "You're going to die when you feel this yarn. And the colors are just amazing."

Luciana followed Lily and lost track of time as she caught on to the enthusiasm at the display of yarn skeins in muted colors.

Finally, they moved to the register, and Luciana paid for her purchases.

"I have to go," Luciana said. "I'm already late for dinner at the DiLorenzos."

"With Paola and Nonna? That will be nice. They're such great cooks," said Lily.

Luciana took the paper shopping bag. "And Jack too. He was the one who invited me today."

Lily and Oliver exchanged a glance.

Luciana paused. "What? Something the matter?"

"It's nice to hear Jack is dating again," Lily said.

"Oh, we're not dating." Luciana's neck heated at the suggestion. "It's just a simple dinner with the family." After all, she was leaving soon. Dating involved more time than what she had—however appealing the idea of it sounded. Somehow, she knew Jack would be a considerate boyfriend.

Lily walked Luciana to the door. "I'm glad to know Jack is back to being social."

Luciana and Oliver said goodbye to Lily, and Luciana walked the two blocks to the DiLorenzo residence, behind the café.

Lily's words remained with her. What had she meant by it? Luciana thought back to all the times she'd spent with Jack and the little she knew about him. How bad had the breakup with his fiancée been for him if he hadn't dated since?

The more she learned about Jack, the more curious she became and the more she wanted to know. Would he let her come closer?

Jack checked the time on the wall clock in the kitchen again. Luciana was late. He'd invited her over for dinner, and she'd said she was coming, but after the winky emoji she'd sent, he wasn't sure of anything anymore.

Was he expecting too much? Or pushing too soon? Maybe admitting that he thought of her all the time hadn't been a good idea; he shouldn't have done it yet. He was trying to be genuine and make his feelings known to Luciana, but her response had been vague. What did a winky emoji mean anyway? Did she feel pressured by his attention? Or did she not know what to say?

Jack scrubbed his face and let out a long sigh. He really had no idea what he was doing. Maybe Luciana had changed her mind about dinner tonight. She hadn't given any indications of such, but could he really trust his own judgment toward women? After his colossal fail with Madison, he didn't know anymore.

Why were relationships so hard? Not that he was in a relationship with Luciana; not a romantic one anyway. He could argue that a friendship was a relationship. It was a good place to start, but he wanted more. How that would work with her living in another country—he couldn't say.

Across the kitchen, in the family room, Mom and Nonna sat on opposing chairs, one reading and the other knitting, as they typically did in the evenings. They'd had dinner already, preferring to eat earlier to accommodate their bedtime.

Nonna put the scarf she knit on her lap, stretched, then stifled a yawn. "Is your girl still coming?"

Jack approached and sat on the edge of the sofa in front of them. "She's not my girl. I haven't heard from her, so I think she's still coming." Or maybe that was him being hopeful.

The doorbell rang and Jack looked up toward the front room.

"That's probably her now," Mom said. "Could you get the door, please?"

As he walked over to the door, Jack flexed his hands, suddenly damp. The nerves took him by surprise.

When he opened the door, his shoulders relaxed, and relief surged through him. Luciana stood there in her red coat—rosy-cheeked, bright-eyed, and absolutely beautiful.

"I'm so sorry I'm late," Luciana said.

Jack's heart skipped a beat. He was so in trouble.

He opened the door wide to let her in. "I'm glad you made it. Come on in."

She entered and kissed him on the cheek, as he'd come to expect from her. Jack closed the door and helped her out of her coat, then hung it up.

Luciana removed her boots and took the guest slippers Mom had left in the entry closet. A crooked smile tugged at the corner of his mouth. It pleased him to see how comfortable Luciana was in his home. She fit right in, as if she'd been coming for years instead of a few days.

She trailed behind him to the kitchen. "I lost track of time. Oliver took me to meet his cousin Lily at her knitting store and that place is amazing."

"You went to Knotty *Kneeters* shop?" Nonna asked with a smile, her accent showing strong.

Luciana greeted Mom and Nonna with kisses on the cheek and took a seat close to Nonna. "Do you go there often? Isn't that place such a gem?" She leaned forward to look at Nonna's lap. "What are you working on? That yarn is fabulous."

Jack busied himself readying the food he'd

prepared earlier, warming the sauce before he mixed it with the ravioli. While he waited, he tossed the winter salad with the vinaigrette.

After a few minutes, he called her. "Dinner is ready."

Nonna put her knitting away, and she and Mom stood. "That's our cue," Mom said.

"You're not staying for dinner?" Luciana asked. "Hope you're not leaving on my account."

"Don't worry. We're not," said Mom.

"We already had the dinner," Nonna asked. "Now it's time for the bed." She placed her palms on her lower back. "These old bones need to rest." She kissed Luciana on both cheeks. *"Buona notte, Luchana."*

"Luciana, what are your plans for Christmas?" Mom asked.

He should have thought of that too.

"Not much. I'm working a half day on Christmas Eve. On Christmas Day, I was going to call my family in the morning and catch up on some personal projects and some reading."

"Come spend it with us," Mom said. "Christmas Eve and Day." She pulled Luciana into a brief hug.

"Thank you, Paola. I'll come," Luciana replied.

Contentment spread through Jack as he heard her reply.

Jack plated the salad first, and Luciana took a seat at the table. "You and your family have been so nice to me," she said, then looked at the contents on the plate. "What are we having?"

"Brussels sprout salad with warm bacon vinaigrette." He set the other plate on the table. "For the main course, pumpkin ravioli with a portobello mushroom filling and a sage, white wine sauce."

Luciana joined her palms and grinned at her plate. "My goodness, Jack. This looks fabulous. Where do you even buy pumpkin ravioli?" She picked up her fork and took a bite.

"I made the pasta from scratch." It was something he enjoyed doing. "The basic pasta recipe is easy, and then I just added pumpkin purée. Or you can add other flavors."

"Mmm," Luciana said. "Wow. I don't have words." She took another slow bite and swallowed. "I'm so going to miss your cooking and baking, Jack DiLorenzo." Her words added to the warm, happy expression on her face.

"I'm so going to miss you, Luciana Romano," Jack replied without hesitation.

Her cheeks colored, and a small smile graced her lips. "I'm going to miss you too. Not just your food." She put her fork down and covered his hand with hers.

Jack turned his hand and squeezed her fingers. "I've really enjoyed spending time with you. I'm glad you're coming for Christmas."

"I'm looking forward to it."

They ate for a few minutes, and Jack liked seeing how much Luciana appreciated the food. In a few more days, she wouldn't be around to have dinner with him. Until then, he'd enjoy every moment he had with her.

Jack took a breath. "When's your flight?"

"On Wednesday the twenty-seventh. It leaves at ten at night."

"It'll be strange when you leave next week." It felt like he'd known her for a lot longer.

She pushed her finished plate away and turned to him with a serious look in her eyes. "When Oliver and Lily Kerrison heard I was coming over for dinner, they mentioned you haven't dated in two years. Not that we're dating," she quickly added.

"Maybe we're not dating, but we have been going on dates," Jack said.

Luciana crossed her arms on the table, as if waiting for him.

Jack sobered, nodding slowly. "They're right. I haven't dated since Madison left. I guess—I guess it affected me. I lost my confidence." Jack rested his elbows on the edge and leaned toward Luciana. She did the same. "It's taken me a while to get to this point, Luciana. I was hurt, and I didn't trust myself or my judgment anymore. But now I'm glad I'm here with you."

Sitting on her right, almost touching, the closeness between them was more than physical, more than space omitted. He wanted this woman to know him—the real him. He was ready for the kind of connection that started with intimate dinners and long conversations, and went beyond that. He wanted to spend more time with her, go on more dates, maybe even kiss her.

His eyes flicked to her lips, and she inhaled quickly, something passing in her expression.

Jack straightened, and the moment broke. It was too soon, wasn't it?

"Next time I see Frank, I'll have to thank him for bringing you over," Jack said.

Luciana smiled. "Who knows where I would have ended up."

"Do you go on dates in Portugal?" Under different circumstances, he wouldn't have asked her, but this time between them had turned more personal, and he didn't want to lose that yet.

"Not since university. I let my life get too busy." She hesitated before going on. "One of the reasons I took this project was to get away from my extended family during the holidays. I have two cousins planning weddings." She flashed him a tight smile. "It's not so easy to be the single one around so much happiness."

"I know that well. With three married sisters with kids, I get a lot of comments about being single."

"I'll be your plus one if you'll be mine," she said with a playful smile.

Jack tightened his grip on her hand for a shake. "Deal."

He smiled. Christmas this year was shaping up to be quite different.

CHAPTER NINE

$\mathcal{B}$ig, fat, fluffy flakes of snow started falling in the midafternoon. White and wet and totally unexpected.

Luciana had not been paying attention to the weather forecast, and when Oliver told her to look out the window, she gasped at the unexpected vision.

Snow. Her first real snowfall. Right outside the museum.

For the rest of the afternoon, she stopped to look out the window often, distracting herself with the serenity of it.

Matt Garrison came by to see the progress and brought fresh sandwiches and drinks for everyone at the museum from a different café in town, and Luciana was glad to show him the exhibit taking form.

When Oliver left the room to fetch some pins to fix a drooping sweater, Matt waited until he was gone, then took a step closer to her.

"I've been meaning to ask you something, and it looks like this is the moment," he said, slipping his hands in his pockets.

Luciana paused and blinked. "Is it about the exhibit? Did you find a mistake in something I did?" Her shoulders tensed.

"No, nothing like that," he rushed to say. "Do you have plans for Christmas? I realize this is kind of short notice, but if you don't have anywhere to go, I'd be happy to have you. It won't just be me," he added. "Some of my family will be there too."

The tightness in her back released and she smiled. "I already got an invitation, but thank you for thinking of me. That's very thoughtful of you."

He nodded with a slow smile. "You're going to the DiLorenzos," he said, stating, not asking.

"Yes, they invited me," she responded.

"You and Jack?" Matt asked, his implication clear. Was that regret in his eyes?

"I think so," she replied. Maybe she was assuming too much, but she liked to think she and Jack had become closer in the past few days.

"Good, good." He cocked his head and raised an eyebrow. "You don't happen to have a sister, do you?" His smile was light, almost boyish.

Luciana chuckled. "No, but I have cousins I'd be happy for you to meet."

Matt shook her hand. "Deal."

She watched him leave. Matt Garrison was a good man and she'd meant what she'd said. Her cousins

Catarina and Jacinta were taken—both almost married—and Susana and Anita were a bit too young for him. But Gabriela and Juliana were still single. If they ever made it to Hudson Springs, she'd gladly introduce one of them to Matt.

By the time she clocked out, a white layer covered everything in view. Several of the downtown businesses had already cleared sidewalks and paths to their doors, working with big shovels and machines that blew the snow out of a sideways tube.

Luciana stood outside the museum doors, feeling the soft snow around her, the quietude that permeated the air, the subtle glow of the lights and colors.

"Let me guess—your first snow?" Oliver asked with a small chuckle.

Luciana raised her face to the sky. "I saw snow at the mountain resort, but this is amazing."

"Come on, I'll give you a ride," he said.

When Oliver dropped her off at the inn, snow still fell softly from the sky. Despite the roads and streets having been cleared recently, as evidenced by the tracks left behind, the accumulation had grown a little. Maybe there would be enough snow on the ground in the morning for Luciana to take some pictures before she left Hudson Springs.

I'll be there in a couple minutes.

Luciana's heart jumped at the text from Jack.

I'm ready, she replied.

Jack had told her he had a surprise this evening. He hadn't given any clues, but she was safe to assume it was something beyond dinner at his home.

When Jack entered the foyer at the inn, Luciana rose from the stuffed chair to meet him. A wide smile appeared on his face, as it always did when he saw her, and she smiled back, happier to see him than she wanted to admit to herself.

She had just seen him yesterday night. His family had invited her over for dinner again. How could she be this happy to see him with barely a day gone by?

Jack lifted a large paper bag. "I brought some stuff."

She reached inside and withdrew a man's parka. "This is for me?"

"It's part of the surprise, not a gift. We'll be outside for a little while, and your coat is not insulated." He gestured inside the bag. "There's also a pair of snow boots I borrowed from my mom. And no, she won't be needing them tonight," he added with a smile, anticipating her question.

Luciana sat on the edge of the chair and traded her fashion boots for the sturdy, warm ones. Then she donned the parka over her coat and pulled the hood over her knit cap. "Okay, I'm ready."

Jack drove north toward the outskirts of town, and they didn't say much, appreciating the comfortable silence between them and the night views of houses decorated with garlands of Christmas lights. Thirty minutes later, Jack turned right on a side road and then passed through the open gates to a long driveway.

"Where are we?" Luciana asked.

"At the Mount Hudson Ski Resort."

"It looks different." Last time, they'd arrived during daylight.

"It's another entrance."

Jack pulled up beside a large barn-like structure and switched off the engine. He turned to Luciana. "I need you to close your eyes before we go in." His enthusiasm was childlike, and she smiled.

"Will you make sure I don't trip? I don't want to fall on the snow."

"Of course." Jack exited and came around the front of the car, then opened the passenger door for her. "Okay, close your eyes and no peeking." He took her by the arm.

Luciana scrunched her eyes closed and concentrated on her steps beside Jack. A door opened ahead, and when they passed inside, the temperature rose a little. From the strong scents and unmistakable sounds of animals breathing and moving around, the place had to be a horse barn. Why had Jack taken her there?

"Do I smell horses? Can I open my eyes yet?"

"Almost," Jack replied. They stopped, and his hands came to rest on her shoulders. "Okay. Now."

She blinked until the view before her was clear. A black- and- red covered sleigh stood in front of them, with lanterns hanging from the sides, and a man holding on to the reins of a brown horse at the front.

Luciana gasped. "A sleigh? A horse-drawn sleigh in the snow?"

Jack's expression fell. "Do you not like it?"

She turned to him with a wide smile. "Are you kidding? I love it!"

His shoulders relaxed, and he took her hand to help her up. "We're going for a ride. As long as the snow stays light, we'll be okay."

The man handed the reins to Jack, and, after an introduction to Luciana and a few last-minute instructions, he opened the wide barn doors and the sleigh slid outside.

"You look like you've done this before," Luciana said to Jack. He held himself confidently, at ease with the horse and the sleigh.

"We used to go for sleigh rides during Christmas break as a family when I was younger, but it's been a while," Jack said.

His jaw tensed for a moment, and Luciana held back a comment. From what he'd told her, she knew his father had been gone for some time, but memories triggered pain on occasions.

Luciana sat back and tightened the scarf around her neck.

Jack passed the reins to one hand and pulled a blanket over her shoulders with his other one. "There's also a lap blanket right here with heated bricks under it."

She bent down and grabbed the heavy blanket, and the banked warmth soon reached her feet and legs. "Now I understand what the heated bricks are for."

Jack glanced at her. "It feels great, doesn't it?"

After a gradual ascent through a country road in the woods, they arrived at a clearing overlooking the town of Hudson Springs. The lights from the buildings and from the Christmas decorations twinkled in the distance, unclear and misty through the light snow. Around them, the night air smelled crisp and sharp, tinged with the vibrancy of fresh pine needles.

And the snow still fell.

Luciana sighed. "This is so wonderful," she said to Jack. "Thank you."

Jack turned to her. His eyes caught the pale light of the lanterns hanging from the sleigh, and his smile warmed his features. "You're welcome. The first snowfall is always magic."

She nodded. "It is. Very different from seeing the ground covered with it."

"I almost forgot." Jack bent and retrieved something from in between the wrapped bricks. "Special DiLorenzo recipe." He handed her a stainless steel mug. "This one's for you." He bent again. "And this one's for me."

"Hot chocolate?" Luciana asked with a smile. She held it between both hands, enjoying the warmth through her knit gloves. Slowly, she twisted the lid to expose the spout.

"Careful, it might still be hot," Jack warned. "Not just any hot chocolate. This is the recipe my Nonno developed. High fat, high calories, very rich taste."

Luciana sipped. It was beyond rich. Creamy, smooth, and not overly sweet. "This is perfect." She tasted it again. "It's not the same recipe you have at the café, is it?"

"We save this one for special occasions."

Did he mean to say this was such an occasion?

The blanket behind her back fell off, and Jack pulled it back up. "You're probably frozen by now."

"Not as much as I'd expected," Luciana replied. "Why don't you get under the blanket with me?"

Even in the low light, Jack's surprised expression was clear. A slow smile grew, and he tilted his head.

Her cheeks heated when she realized what she'd said. "Oh goodness." She covered her mouth with her gloved hand. "That was so not what I meant."

"Relax, Luciana." He put down his mug, then scooted closer to her. With his other hand, he lifted the corner of the blanket until they were both covered. Luciana tightened the fabric on her side, and before she gave it much thought, she pressed next to him. Immediately, Jack's arm went around her shoulder, and he brought her closer to his side.

He took a deep breath. "This is much better. Thanks for suggesting it," he added in a light, teasing tone.

Under the canopy of the sleigh, wrapped in blankets and with the heated bricks, and the delicious hot chocolate still in her hand, Luciana could only agree with Jack. The warmth of his body next to hers brought a sense of contentment beyond her physical comfort at the moment. Her heart swelled with feelings she'd been putting off for a long time. She found Jack's hand, then squeezed his fingers.

She knew the moment something shifted between them. An energy pulsed, strong and undeniable. Jack's other hand dropped to her waist, and he turned her to face him, closing the distance even more. Their breaths mingled for a short moment, until their lips met.

His kiss was tentative at first—probing, pulling away, going back.

Cold skin. Warm lips. Fire and ice.

Luciana lost her patience. She put down her mug and wound her arms around Jack's neck, deepening the kiss. The rich taste of chocolate intensified in her mouth, and a wave of warmth spread through her.

Jack moaned.

Everything around them became secondary. Just the feel of his lips, the warm skin at the back of his neck, his taste, his scent.

Maybe it lasted for a few minutes, or maybe for just an eternal moment. In time, they slowed down to only little kisses, still clinging to each other.

"Luciana." Jack's voice was low, almost ragged, the emotion exposed.

What could she say? What could she possibly say that would do justice to what had just happened between them?

Luciana dropped her arms from around his neck and held on to his hands. "I'm leaving soon." Deep breath. "I only have five days, Jack." She glanced away.

How could she have kissed him with such wild abandon when they had such little time?

Jack rolled the car into the garage and turned off the engine. He sat there thinking about the evening. Thinking about Luciana and the amazing kiss they'd shared. He hadn't planned for it, and, judging by Luciana's response, she'd been surprised as well. But, wow ... Such passion. How was he supposed to forget it and keep going as before?

They didn't talk much on the drive back. Luciana had tried to keep things light, but there was still too much tension—an energy between them that was hard to ignore. And like she'd said, she was leaving soon.

The extended forecast called for heavier snow the day after Christmas. If it kept up, would she be able to leave on time? And if she didn't, what would that mean for them?

Jack exited the car, put on his insulated boots, and picked up the snow shovel. If he got a head start clearing tonight, it would be easier in the morning. He had other people who depended on him to shovel their driveways and sidewalks as well, and little time to do it.

By the time he came in the house from the garage, Mom waited at the table with a cup of hot chocolate.

She handed him a mug. "How did it go?"

He sat down and took a sip, buying some time. "Good. It went pretty well." Jack nodded and sipped again.

What could he say? That he'd broken the promise he'd made himself after the Madison fiasco? To keep away from women? And now he'd gone and kissed Luciana. Not a little peck. A real kiss—one that shook him to his core.

Mom eyed him sideways, almost like she could read his mind, which he didn't doubt she could at times.

"Is it her first snowfall?" Mom asked.

Jack smiled a little. "Yes, it is. You should have seen her face." He wouldn't be forgetting Luciana's expression any time soon.

"Did you tell her about the weather forecast? It calls for heavy snow on the twenty-sixth."

"I didn't get the chance to bring it up." He'd been busy kissing her instead of warning her about the weather. "I'll talk to her."

Mom nodded. "All right. Let's wait and see how the weather is. Maybe it won't be as bad as we think." She stood and took her cup to the sink. "Good night."

Jack made his way to bed a few minutes later. Through the open slats in the blinds of his bedroom window, the snow fell in solid flakes. When he checked the weather app again, the snowstorm rolling in on Monday now covered most of the area, expected to move on by the weekend. For sure, the airports would close, and they wouldn't be the only ones.

One thing at a time. First, he needed a few hours of sleep. Then, he'd get up earlier to make extra dough in preparation to bake more bread for those in need. He might as well attach the plow to his truck since the shovel wouldn't be enough to do the work.

He rolled to his back and took a deep breath. What would bring sleep faster—thoughts of Luciana, or pushing her out of his mind?

When the alarm on the cell phone rang three hours later, Jack reached for it and turned it off. He sat up in bed and rubbed a hand over his face. A long breath escaped his mouth, more like a weary sigh for another night with not enough sleep. His shoulders slumped at the view outside his window—the snow still fell like before. It would be a long day.

Jack turned the phone in his hand, half-expecting, half-hoping for a text from Luciana, but there was nothing. How much work did she have today and tomorrow morning? She'd mentioned she was only working the morning of Christmas Eve, but if the snow continued, maybe he could convince her to come to them earlier.

The concern for Luciana raised in his heart. How was she really doing about being away from her family at Christmastime? They'd had the chance for plenty of conversation by now and Jack knew how close her family was. He'd heard of the holidays spent with cousins and grandparents, how fun and special those days were. She'd taken this trip on purpose, to get away and spare her feelings, but that didn't mean she wouldn't regret it when the time came and she discovered how different his family was.

What could he do to help her deal with her emotions? And how would she react if the snowstorm closed down the airport?

His stomach churned, heavy with guilt. The prospect of spending more time with her excited him, but she might not feel the same way.

CHAPTER TEN

$\mathcal{L}$uciana arrived at the DiLorenzo's Bakery and Café just before noon and stomped her boots on the rug by the door. She brushed her coat, shaking off as much of the snow as possible before entering. Maybe she should have listened to Mr. Wynthrop at the museum. Instead of the usual seven minutes, it took her over twenty to walk the one-and-a-half blocks between the two buildings. The most labored walk of her life. Who knew walking in the snow could be so hard? She'd returned the oversized coat and heavy boots Jack had lent her the night before, and what she wore was sadly inappropriate. Underestimating the short distance in heavy snow conditions hadn't been a smart idea. She trembled as the cold in her feet seeped and spread through the rest of her body.

After the sleighride and the kiss she'd shared with Jack, Luciana hadn't been thinking straight, and asking pertinent questions about the forecast didn't even cross her mind. She'd tossed and turned all night, unable to set her body to rest, unwilling to get her mind on something else. Instead, she relived those moments with Jack, over and over again, until she fell into a fitful sleep in the early morning only to wake up a few hours later.

Paola DiLorenzo met her at the door. "Luciana, what are you doing out in this weather? Did you walk here?"

Luciana let the coat fall off her shoulders, and Jack's mom caught it.

"I had a break for lunch," Luciana replied. Her teeth chattered and she closed her mouth firmly. She pulled off her cap and gloves but didn't move. The snow on her boots was melting rapidly, and she didn't want to track the water puddle on the wood floor. She winced. "I'm getting the floor all wet, Mrs. DiLorenzo." Her chin quivered in between words.

"Please, call me Paola. And don't worry about the floor."

Luciana slid her feet out of the utterly useless fashion boots, and Paola picked them up, carrying them in her other hand.

"Come with me," Paola said. "We need to get you changed from those wet clothes into something warm."

Luciana didn't argue, unable to think past the feeling of pins and needles in her feet as the heat warmed her blood. She absently noticed that the café was empty, and Jack wasn't around. Where was he?

Somehow, she found the strength to follow Paola to the back of the café and up the stairs that connected to the house.

Paola opened the door to a bedroom, and Luciana sat on the edge of the bed. After a few minutes, Paola returned with a stack of clothes.

"There are towels in the bathroom closet. Come to the living room when you're ready. I'll put your clothes in the dryer."

Jack's nonna already sat by the fireplace when Luciana entered the living room some time later. The clickety-clack of the metal needles as the old woman knit was a soothing, relaxing sound. Luciana had taken a quick shower and changed into the lounge clothes, including a thick pair of socks and a well-loved chunky cardigan.

Nonna paused and raised her head. "You feeling warm now?"

Luciana's cheeks heated, embarrassment coursing through her. She nodded. "I'm feeling better. Thank you." She shouldn't have walked in the snow without being better prepared.

Paola returned with a cup in hand. "This will perk you up, Luciana."

Luciana took the cup, the chocolate scent already familiar to her. She chose the overstuffed chair closer to the fire, and tucked her legs to the side. Outside the windows, the snow fell in white droves, not intensely yet, but showing no signs of slowing down. She sipped, mesmerized at the scene.

"Did you have nice time with Jack last night?" Nonna asked.

Luciana choked, and a blush warmed her cheeks. She put down the cup and wiped the hot chocolate from her mouth. "Jack was great. I mean, we had a great time." If the best kiss of her life could be described as great. "The sleighride was very nice," she added, trying to push away the memories of Jack's lips on her.

The old lady smiled, as if she knew what had happened between Jack and Luciana. Maybe Nonna could see it on Luciana's expression.

"Where is Jack, by the way?" Luciana asked. "I didn't see him at the café."

Just then, Paola reentered the living room. "Jack has been delivering bread and clearing driveways since early this morning."

"It hasn't stopped snowing. How can he get anything done?" With so much snow coming down, Luciana wondered how much progress he actually made.

"He has a shovel for hard to reach places, but also a snowblower and a plow attachment on his truck." Paola proceeded to explain the various ways to clean out the snow.

"Wouldn't it be easier to remove the snow after it's done snowing?"

"He'll have to do that too, but the snow is softer before it freezes." Paola left the room and returned a few minutes later with a plate carrying a sandwich and a variety of small pastries, which she set on the coffee table. "It's nice to see the color back in your cheeks. You looked so pale when you walked in."

"I should have brought a bigger coat and snow boots. Maybe Jack can give me a ride back to the museum?"

Paola looked up. "Why are you going back to the museum?"

"I'm supposed to work today and tomorrow morning," Luciana told them.

Paola shook her head. "I doubt they'll keep the museum open, especially with Christmas coming and the weather like this."

"More snow is coming," Jack's grandma said.

"Mamma is right. The forecast calls for snow until Christmas morning, partly cloudy on Tuesday, and then more snow coming on Wednesday afternoon."

Luciana looked between them. "But that's when I'm leaving. On Wednesday night. How bad will it get?"

"According to the forecast, there might be some road closures, but we'll have to see how it turns out," Paola replied.

Luciana's phone rang with an incoming call with the museum's phone number. "Excuse me. I need to take this."

She walked toward the foyer and answered the phone. "This is Luciana."

"Luciana, this is Augustus Wynthrop. Mr. Garrison called, and given the current weather conditions, we decided to close the museum until after Christmas."

"Oh," she said, sitting down on the closest chair. "I still have quite a bit of work to finish before I leave."

"We're aware of that. Let's plan on meeting on Tuesday the twenty-sixth in the morning. What do you say?"

"I'll be there," she replied.

Mr. Wynthrop wished her Merry Christmas, and Luciana returned the greeting, then walked back to the back of the house.

She took the same chair. "That was Mr. Wynthrop, the museum director. They decided to close earlier, and I don't have to go back in until Tuesday," she told Paola and Nonna.

"You stay here with us," Nonna said. She tugged at the yarn in a basket by the side of the sofa.

Paola leaned forward in her chair. "Yes, stay with us. You were already coming tomorrow for Christmas Eve."

"I was planning on bringing an overnight bag." She only had her phone with her.

"If the weather lets up, Jack can give you a ride to the inn. If not, we'll lend you what you need," Paola said. She excused herself and returned to the café.

Nonna continued knitting, and Luciana remained silent for a moment, considering the situation. She'd been counting on working today and tomorrow morning and worried about the unfinished project. Hopefully she'd be able to catch up when the museum reopened after Christmas.

In the meantime, she needed something to do while she stayed at the DiLorenzos, especially her personal knitting projects and the stash of yarn she'd bought at The Knotty Knitters.

Until Jack returned, she could get started on planning and sketching the extra projects.

Jack entered the house and found Mom, Nonna, and Luciana in the living room. Nonna was knitting, and Mom had old photo albums on the coffee table as she showed family photos to Luciana.

"You're here," he said to Luciana. "Hi."

She smiled back and blushed lightly.

"Luciana came for lunch, but then the museum closed, and we invited her to stay," Mom said.

He reined in his grin, cutting it back into a small smile. Looking too happy about it would be rude. "That makes sense."

"I don't have to go back to work until Tuesday morning," Luciana said.

He shouldn't be so happy about it, but he was. She'd be here for two extra days.

"Any chance you could give me a ride to the inn?" Luciana asked.

His shoulders slumped. "So you're not staying?"

"I am. I just need to pack a few things."

He nodded. "Of course." He glanced at the wall clock. "Let's go now before the weather gets worse."

After borrowing his mom's coat and boots, Luciana climbed into the truck with his help, and he left slowly. In fair weather, the drive wouldn't take more than five minutes, but today he had to be careful and patient.

"Thanks for the ride," Luciana said. "I'm sorry you had to come back out."

"You're welcome. Don't worry about it," he replied. "It'll give me a chance to check on Mrs. Wells and see if she needs anything.

Mrs. Wells employed a snow removal service to clear the driveways and the inn's small parking lot, but he'd feel better to see how she was doing.

Jack dropped off Luciana in the back and was pleased to see the paths and driveways had been cleared earlier. Of course, with the snow still falling, there would be more to do in the morning.

He entered the kitchen and found Mrs. Wells there, stirring a big pot of hot chocolate.

"How are you, Mrs. Wells?" Jack stood by the door, letting the snow melt off his boots onto to the rug. "Do you have everything you need to ride the storm?"

She looked at him, still holding on to the pot and wooden spoon. "Thanks for asking, Jack. Will you be making fresh bread in the morning?"

"I will. How much do you need?"

"It's just me and a couple that decided to leave after Christmas. Maybe two loaves?"

"Any croissants or pastries?" he asked.

"Whatever you can spare will be fine. Luciana said

she's spending Christmas with your family," she added with a small smile.

"Yes, my mother and grandmother invited her." Why did the kitchen feel so hot?

"I'm sure you let Luciana feel welcome too," Mrs. Wells said.

Jack shifted his weight. "Of course." Where was Luciana?

Just then she entered the kitchen pulling a small suitcase. "There. It only took me five minutes. Thanks for waiting."

That was all? It sure felt much longer.

Luciana kissed Mrs. Wells' cheek. "I left a little something under the tree for you. Merry Christmas."

Mrs. Wells pulled Luciana into a quick hug. "You're too kind, dear. Have a wonderful time."

Why did Mrs. Wells look at him when she said that?

When they arrived back at the house, Luciana took her luggage to the guest bedroom, and Jack went to his to take a shower.

Once again, Luciana filled his thoughts. They hadn't talked much on the drive to the inn and back, but it hadn't been exactly the right moment for it.

How did she feel to be here a day earlier? It would be easier to find opportunities to spend more time together. He'd just have to foster these moments before his sisters and their families arrived. There would be no privacy after.

When he returned downstairs, Mom was on the phone with one of his sisters, and Nonna had gone to her bedroom for her afternoon nap. He placed the covered plate Mom had left for him in the microwave, then walked to the living room where Luciana sat by the fireplace. She had her phone in her hand and a small frown between her eyebrows.

He sat on the chair across from her. "Everything okay?"

"I'm just checking the extended forecast." She looked up from the screen to him, some hesitancy in her expression. "Your grandma invited me to stay when the museum closed earlier. Is that okay with you?"

"Absolutely." His heart leaped in his chest, and Jack scooted to the back of his chair, trying to put some distance between him and Luciana. "We'll be glad to have you here. You were already coming for Christmas Eve."

"That's what your mom said." She bit her bottom lip. "I just—just wanted to make sure my being here won't make things awkward between us."

The microwave beeped, and Jack walked to the kitchen. "Of course not," he said over his shoulder.

Did she think he didn't want her to stay because of the kiss? They hadn't talked about it, but it was obviously on her mind, just as it was on his. It had been in the back of his mind all night and all day.

Luciana put the phone in her pocket and followed him, waiting until he got his plate out. Jack uncovered it and took a fork from the utensils drawer. "Did you eat yet?"

She nodded. "Your mom fed me when I got here."

Jack pulled out a chair at the table for Luciana, then took a seat across from her. "It's only awkward if we make it so," he said, then took a bite. "I'm glad Nonna invited you." He hoped to put Luciana at ease, because he really was glad she was there.

Her expression relaxed, her cheeks a little more pink than usual. "I'm glad too."

This was new for them, and they both knew it. Jack hadn't been planning on meeting a woman who caught his interest in this manner, and Luciana had come on a business trip. Whatever this wonderful thing was between them, he wanted more of it, and he was ready to see where it went.

Luciana propped her chin on her hand. "Your mom mentioned you were delivering bread this morning?"

"I baked some extra bread to hand out to whomever needs it, especially if they're older friends and neighbors who live alone. We just make sure they're set up to ride the storm, and have enough food and water and heating." He shrugged between bites. "Since I have a plow attachment for the truck and snowblower, clearing the driveways and sidewalks doesn't take too long." He didn't want to make a big deal out of it.

She nodded. "Your mother explained about the snow freezing."

"It won't be as easy after it stops snowing, that's for sure."

"That's good of you to take time to help those people." Her tone was warm, almost with a hint of admiration.

Jack rushed to change the subject. "Did you call your family?"

"I talked to my mom, and she was worried about me, but I told her I met an awesome family who took me in." Her lips quirked in a smile.

He rinsed his plate and placed it in the dishwasher. "The qualities of this family might be slightly exaggerated," he said, unable to keep from teasing. "You can tell your mom we'll keep you anytime, not just at Christmas." He meant it, wishing she could stay longer, wishing they could have more time beyond the holidays to get to know each other.

Luciana's expression softened and she looked at him as if she were trying to figure him out. "Can I ask you a question?" she asked.

"Anything you want," he replied. Jack didn't want to hold back from Luciana. Her limited time in Hudson Springs didn't leave any room for the usual dating games, like the ones Madison had pulled him into. That should have been a red flag back then, but his distraction with her had left him blind to the warning signs.

He wouldn't make the same mistake with Luciana.

"Do you still have feelings for your ex-fiancée?" she asked.

Jack stilled, surprised by Luciana's directness, then took a step closer. "Do you think I would have kissed you like I did yesterday if I still felt anything for her?"

Luciana held his gaze.

They stood close enough that he could see the color variations in her brown eyes. They weren't solid brown, like he'd previously thought. A lighter ring surrounded the pupil before diffusing into the perfect chocolate hue.

"I don't go about kissing men like that either," she replied in a soft tone. Her cheeks colored briefly.

"Good." He took her hand and rubbed the inner spot of her wrist.

Luciana held her breath.

"Now we understand each other." His tone matched hers, almost as if they shared secrets no one else knew.

At the sound of Mom descending the staircase, Jack squeezed Luciana's fingers and put some distance between them.

"Jack, I just talked to your sisters," Mom said on her way to the kitchen. "Let's plan the menus."

"I'll be right there," he replied more loudly.

Luciana leaned back against the kitchen counter, watching him.

He took two steps, then turned back until he stood in front of her like before. "Can we talk more later?"

Luciana swallowed, then nodded slowly. An energy pulsed between them, and when her eyes dipped to his mouth, Jack barely held back from taking her in his arms and kissing her again.

Hours later, after dinner was done and the clean dishes put away, Jack brewed a pot of tea, then sat in the living room by the glow of the fire, the Christmas tree providing the only light. Mom and Nonna had gone to bed, and he waited for Luciana. They hadn't had a private moment since earlier, and he took the few minutes to put his thoughts in order.

When Luciana arrived, she sat at the other end of the sofa instead of taking one of the chairs. She wore flannel pajama bottoms and a knit cardigan over a T-shirt, woolen socks on her feet—most likely handknit—and no slippers. She tucked her legs to the side, and her pant leg rode up, allowing Jack a glimpse of a bit of lace on the cuff of the sock.

He rose and retrieved the tea from the kitchen, handing one of the mugs to Luciana.

"It's a calming blend of herbal tea with a drop of honey," he said. "I find it relaxes me after a harried day."

"Tea?"

Maybe he'd presumed too much. "I'm sorry. I should have asked you if you like herbal tea."

"I love herbal tea," she said, taking a sip. She closed her eyes and savored for a moment. "I think I recognize the flavor."

"It's chamomile and lemon balm. In Italy, it's called *Melissa*."

"They call it the same in Spain, and we have that herb in Portugal as well. It grows everywhere, and it's a popular natural remedy for all sorts of malaise." She sipped again. "I'll have to try it with chamomile. This is very good. Thank you."

"You're welcome. Are Portuguese people tea drinkers then?"

"We sure are," she replied with a smile. "I'll have you know that King Charles the second of England married the Portuguese Catarina de Bragança and she turned tea drinking into a fashionable beverage for the British." She quirked an eyebrow and stretched her pinkie, an amused smile on her lips.

"I did not know that. Actually, I must confess I didn't know much about Portugal, other than the general location." He'd been researching the country a bit more since meeting her.

She put her mug down on the coffee table. "We Portuguese are very proud of our national heritage and influence in the world, so you'll probably learn a few more useless facts before I leave," she said in a light tone.

Was it selfish of him to hope she could stay a few more days? "I have a confession," he said, turning to her.

"What's that?" Luciana lowered her voice.

"I'm glad you're staying with us for a few extra days."

If the storm kept up, maybe she'd stay even longer.

CHAPTER ELEVEN

"You're not the only one. I'm glad too," Luciana admitted.

As inconvenient as the snow was, she hoped the weather wouldn't set her work back too much. With Catarina and Afonso's wedding on January first, Luciana had wanted more free time and didn't have a new project starting until the middle of the month. But she did want to be back in time for the wedding. Hopefully, she could get both of her wishes.

In the end, would extra time make a difference between her and Jack? Was it possible to get to know someone in a couple of weeks? Jacinta and Knox had proved the theory well, but they were the exception, not the rule. More than anything, she wanted to believe her stay at the DiLorenzos had a purpose—one that made her heart speed up with anticipation.

Jack smiled at her reply and reached to give her hand a squeeze. He released it too quickly, and she missed the warmth of his skin against hers.

Luciana shifted in her corner of the sofa and sat crosslegged, facing him more fully. Outside, it snowed on, but in here, the coziness had her wishing they had all night to stay like this, talking and enjoying each other's company. Maybe even kissing again.

Jack sat closer. For a flash, his expression filled with weariness, but he quickly dispelled it.

Was it crazy she wanted to touch him and comfort him? It felt right. Her heart jumped eagerly, and she willed it to calm down. Jack would think her crazy for sure if she threw herself into his arms. How could her heart want one thing while her mind told her something different?

"I want to tell you about what happened between Madison and me. She grew up here in town," he started. "She was three years younger than me, so I didn't notice her much when we were in high school. I came back after Dad passed away, and not much later she returned to help her mom through cancer treatments. We started talking, first at the café when she came in for bread and pastries, and pretty soon, we were meeting almost every day. Dating came after."

That wasn't so different from how he and Luciana had met, was it? Only Luciana was a stranger, a foreigner. There was nothing in common between them.

He paused, and Luciana waited until he was ready to resume.

"During a particularly bad period in her illness, her mother hinted at how she would like to see Madison married, in case something happened, and two weeks later I proposed." Jack scrubbed his face. "Madison's mom had a miraculous recovery, and when Madison received a job offer in Los Angeles a few months later, she took it. She broke up with me before leaving. On Christmas Day."

Luciana leaned forward. "Wait. She broke up with you on Christmas day?"

Jack nodded slowly. "She had a flight early the next morning and thought it best 'to leave everything taken care of', in her own words."

"How awful of her," she replied. She couldn't think of anything else to say that wouldn't sound mean toward Madison. At one point in Jack's life, this woman had meant something to him and Luciana didn't want to add to his pain with her opinion, especially when she didn't have the right to judge the situation.

"The timing wasn't the greatest, but she knew I wouldn't leave Mom and Nonna, and I wouldn't ask her to stay. I haven't dated since then, and I haven't missed it." He sat closer and took her hand. "Until now."

The small hairs at the nape of her neck rose at once, and her pulse sped up. Once again, the feeling of rightness warmed her as a wave radiated from her chest to other parts of her. Almost as if her body wanted her to ingrain the feelings into her heart.

Was this a simple physical attraction, or was there more to it? And how could she know for sure?

Luciana leaned closer again, reducing the distance between them and making it easier to hold hands. "Thank you for telling me," she said.

He was going to kiss her. The intention was there in his eyes, the way they flicked to her face and lips. Her skin prickled, and her cheeks heated. When his mouth touched hers, sweetly and softly, she closed her eyes, and her whole body relaxed, focused on the single act and nothing more.

After a moment, Jack straightened.

"Would you like to help me cook tomorrow?" he asked, standing from the sofa.

That was it? If it weren't for the easy expression on his face, Luciana would have believed she'd imagined the closeness and the kiss, light as it had been. She wanted more, deeper, stronger, and felt strangely cheated.

His question effectively cooled her down, raising a wall. He must have seen the disappointment in her eyes and the surprise in her expression.

"Luciana, if I keep sitting with you on that couch, I'll kiss you senseless all night." He held her hand.

A slow smile formed on her lips. "Well, since you put it that way." It wouldn't be fair to be disappointed, not with such clear words from him. Maybe she wouldn't have minded the kissing-all-night part, as long as they could keep it to kissing and nothing more.

Jack chuckled, a soft, low rumble that had Luciana wishing for things she never had before. She swallowed, trying to understand her feelings.

Didn't Avó Teresa sometimes say that the best things in life were unplanned? Luciana had come to Hudson Springs to work, nothing more. And here she was, attracted to a man she didn't know well, and secretly glad she had a legitimate reason to stay with his family and get to know him more. If her cousins could see her now, they'd tease her, for sure.

But the question remained—what would happen when she left?

She followed Jack as he went around the house locking the doors and windows. The wind and snow had picked up in force. So different from everything she'd ever experienced. After Christmas, she'd have to call the airline and get an update on her flight.

They climbed the stairs, and Jack walked with her to her bedroom door. Luciana opened the door and stood at the entrance as he leaned against the jamb.

"When was the last time you had a boyfriend?" he asked in a low voice.

His mother and grandmother's bedrooms must be close by. It would be awkward for Luciana and Jack to get caught whispering by her bedroom door.

"I've never had a boyfriend," she whispered back. "Not for real, anyway. I've dated some, but I mostly keep busy with my job." That was her official excuse, the one she used to satisfy the curiosity of her family. The Romanos could be such a nosy lot.

In truth, she'd never felt the kind of attraction that led her to seek a second or third date. With all the traveling and research she had to do for work, time was hard to come by, and spending it on guys who didn't understand her had not appealed to her before. But she'd always missed having a connection with someone.

It had taken a trip to New York and an unplanned visit to a local café to give her the opportunity to slow down and get to know a man she was interested in. One who was also interested in her.

What could come of it when they lived on different continents?

SUNDAY, DECEMBER 24TH

Jack didn't remember his dreams, but Luciana was the first thought in his mind when he woke up.

Despite a short night, he still rose early to clean up the snow and check on several people. The weather forecast called for clear skies by Christmas Day in the evening, with a chance of more snow later in the week. What this meant for Luciana, he still didn't know. He'd take it one day at a time and enjoy what they had while it lasted.

By the time she came down for breakfast, he and Mom were in the middle of checking their lists and menus. Nonna sat in the adjacent living room, catching up with some last-minute knitting.

Luciana took a stool at the island. "I wanted to wake up early and help, and instead I slept through the alarm."

Her hair looked like she'd ran her fingers through it, still tousled from bed in plenty of spots, and her right shoulder was bare, the pajama top askew on her frame. Jack stared at her, and when Mom cleared her throat, he dropped his pen on the floor.

Luciana smiled at him, her cheeks tinged with a slight blush.

"Don't worry about it," Mom said. "There's lots to do for today and tomorrow. You'll get a chance to help. But first, breakfast. Would you like me to scramble a couple of eggs for you?"

"No, thank you," Luciana said. "I'm not used to such heavy breakfasts in the morning. A piece of toast will do."

"Are you sure? It won't take long to do it."

"It's what I usually have when I'm at home," Luciana replied.

Mom removed the loaf from the bread box and cut a thick slice, which she placed in the toaster. "Would you like some milk?"

Luciana nodded. "How many people are you expecting tonight?" she asked.

Mom tucked her list in the pocket of her apron. "My daughters usually spend Christmas Day with us, but because of the storm, Amy won't be able to come until Saturday. Kate and Leah will be here for Christmas dinner tomorrow night, I hope." Mom gathered her family recipes. "I'll go get started on the *pandoro*."

After Mom left, Luciana finished her breakfast and took the small plate and glass to the sink.

Jack looked up from his menu. "You don't have to do that, Luciana. I'll be running the dishwasher soon."

"It's okay." She quickly washed them and placed them on the drying rack. "I'm going to take a quick shower and get more presentable."

When she returned twenty minutes later, she joined him at the table. She wore a sweater and jeans and the same slippers Mom had handed to her.

"Where did your mother go?" she asked

"To the kitchen in the café. We make quite a few pandoro, and the big mixer helps to get the dough started while I prep in here."

"What's a pandoro?"

Jack stopped and pushed the laptop away from him. "It means *golden bread* in Italian. It's a sweet yeast bread popular around Christmas, baked in an eight-pointed star-shaped pan and dusted with vanilla-flavored powdered sugar. You can serve it with fruit spreads, fresh fruit, mascarpone cheese, dark chocolate, or whipped cream."

"That sounds delicious," Luciana replied with an interested expression.

"It's a tradition. We can't have Christmas without pandoro. What kind of traditions do you have in Portugal?"

"It depends on the region. The food and dishes vary so much from north to south, and from the interior to the coast. One of my favorites when the Romanos get together is sweet rice." Her eyes lit up.

"How do you make this rice dish?"

"My grandmother and aunts make it, and it's the best. You take short grain rice and cook it in milk seasoned with lemon peels and cinnamon sticks, with sugar and egg yolks, and then you dust it with ground cinnamon." Her eyes closed. "Hmmm. Just thinking about it." She opened her eyes and smiled at him. "For us, it can't be Christmas without sweet rice. Why do you think so many traditions are linked to food?"

"Because food and family go together, and the tastes and smells bring you back to those moments you shared with your loved ones," Jack said. It was the same with his family, the memories and traditions connected to the dishes they loved. "Do you have the recipe? It sounds pretty easy to make."

"Do you have all the ingredients?"

"We sure do." Between their private pantry and the café's, he probably had the best-stocked kitchen in town. Not that he would tell her that—it would sound too much like bragging.

Her face split in a grin. "I'll go call my grandmother Teresa and get the recipe from her."

Jack rose and walked to the pantry to gather the arborio rice, sugar, and cinnamon sticks. He retrieved the eggs from the refrigerator and the lemons from the corner on the counter.

When Luciana returned, she held a piece of paper in her hand. "Step-by-step instructions. The only problem is, last time I tried to make it at home by myself, I managed to botch it."

"I'll help you. It sounds like it's a kind of sweet risotto. You'll have to translate though." He winked at her. "It's in metric, right? We'll need a kitchen scale."

Jack pulled the small scale from a cupboard in the island, and he worked with Luciana to weigh all the ingredients into different bowls. Then they measured the water and milk into a pot with a dash of salt, and he turned the burner on.

"Are your sisters coming alone?"

"My sisters are married with children, so we'll have a full house. Amy has three kids, in their pre-teen and young teen years. Kate has three also, and Leah has four, including a new baby girl."

Luciana's expression bloomed in a large smile. "My cousin Catarina had a baby girl in October. She's the first grandbaby in the family, and we're all so excited. I can't wait to see her."

"So your brothers are not married?" Jack asked.

"Filipe is five years older than me, and he's not married. Paulo is two years younger than me, and Ricardo two years younger than Paulo, and they're students at the university. They date sometimes, but nothing serious."

"And you have cousins getting married soon," he said.

Luciana chuckled. "I do. Two of them—Catarina and her fiancé Afonso on January first and Matias and his fiancée in June. Jacinta and her boyfriend Knox are getting more serious, so I wouldn't be surprised to see them getting married soon as well."

Jack stirred the rice and followed the instructions Luciana read to him.

"We're going to need individual dessert bowls or a ramekin-type of dish," she said.

He walked to the far cabinet and lifted a dessert bowl. "Will something like this do?"

"Perfect," she replied.

Jack grabbed a tray and transferred a dozen of the small bowls to the counter next to the stove.

Luciana ladled the sweet rice into the bowls, placing them back on the tray after filling them. "Now we decorate with ground cinnamon." She poured some into a small plate.

"Show me how," Jack said.

She pinched some cinnamon and leaned close to one of the bowls. "The trick is to move your thumb and your index finger and sprinkle the cinnamon into a pattern. I'm really bad at this, so I just sprinkle it all over." She finished decorating the bowl and shook the excess spice from her fingers over the sink. "My mom and grandmother can do intricate designs."

Jack took a pinch. "I'll give it a try." He worked the cinnamon over the sweet rice, but the result was sloppy. "This is a lot harder than it looks."

Luciana laughed. "Yes, I know."

"I think I got something that might work better," Jack said. He washed his hands and walked to the hall that led to the café. "I'll be right back."

When he returned with the small box of stencils, Luciana raised an eyebrow. "What do you have there?"

Jack opened the box and looked for a stencil that fit the inside of the bowl. "Christmas stencils," he replied. "Now I just need to find the small mesh sieve." He found it, took some cinnamon and poured it in, then shook it over the stencil. When he lifted the stencil, the Christmas tree design on the sweet rice looked festive. "What do you think?"

"My grandma would call it cheating, but I like it." She spread out the stencils on the counter, and soon they had all the bowls of sweet rice decorated.

"What's the best way to eat this?" Jack asked.

Luciana grabbed two small spoons and handed him one along with a bowl. "I like it warm, like it is right now." She lifted the spoon to her mouth. "It tastes just like I remember."

Jack dipped the spoon into his cup and took a bite, savoring the rice. "The spice from the cinnamon, the freshness of the lemon." He ate another spoonful. "The creaminess of the custard in the rice is my favorite."

"Exactly my favorite part," Luciana said, smiling wide.

"Looks like I passed the test," Jack said.

She raised an eyebrow. "What test?"

"You were waiting to see if I liked your sweet rice," he said, unable to keep the smile from his voice any longer. "What do you call it in Portuguese?"

"A-rroz do-ce." Luciana sounded out the syllables.

Jack repeated the words, and she smiled. "The accent needs a little work, but not bad."

He put down his bowl and stepped closer to Luciana. "I like the a-rroz doce." He placed a hand on her waist. "But I like you more."

"Perfect answer, Jack."

Luciana leaned toward him and kissed him on the lips.

Cinnamon and a hint of lemon.

He was such a goner for her.

CHAPTER TWELVE

Monday, December 25th ~ morning

Luciana's cell phone rang as soon as daylight crept through the window. She reached for it and swiped at the screen without looking at the caller ID. She'd stayed up late knitting a cap for Jack, but had barely had the presence of mind to put the needles away before falling asleep without finishing it. She'd have to find the time before she left.

"Hello?" she spoke to the phone.

"You're speaking English, Luciana," her mom said.

Her mom's voice effectively woke Luciana and she sat up in bed. "*Olá, mãe,*" she replied in Portuguese. "I've been speaking English since I arrived here. It's a habit. How are you?"

"*Feliz Natal,*" a group of voices shouted over the phone.

Merry Christmas indeed. She smiled. It was Christmas morning and she'd almost forgotten.

She returned the greeting and laughed. "Who's there?"

"Hi, Luciana. How are you?"

Her brothers took turns greeting her, and she smiled, glad to hear their voices on Christmas morning. A pang of longing squeezed her heart. It was the first time away from home on Christmas. She'd made the decision to come to New York on purpose, but she'd thought she'd be all right with it. Now, so far away from her family, she missed them more than she'd anticipated.

After talking to Filipe, Paulo, and Ricardo, Dad got on the phone for a few minutes before passing it back to Mom.

"We're leaving to Avô António and Avó Teresa's in a few minutes," Mom said.

The extended family usually got together for lunch at the grandparents' home. Anyone who could make the trip would be there.

Luciana missed them all.

"You're not spending Christmas Day alone, are you?" Mom asked.

Luciana wiped her silent tears, keeping her voice even and bright. "No, I'm not alone. I'm spending it with the DiLorenzos."

"The ones who own the café?"

"Yes. It's Jack and his mom and grandma. Two of his sisters and their families will arrive later today," Luciana said. "It's been snowing a lot, and traveling is kind of hard."

"Are you still leaving on Wednesday night?" Mom asked.

"That will depend on the airport closures, but I'll keep you updated. When is everyone going down to Castelo Branco for the wedding?"

"Your aunts Glória, Mariana, and Celestina are leaving on Saturday to get a start on the food. Almost everyone else is going on Sunday," Mom replied. "Just make sure you're not late."

"I won't be," Luciana assured. "I'm not missing this wedding for anything."

"And the baby's christening."

"I'll not miss that either since I'm the godmother. You should see the little outfit I knit for Carlota." Luciana described the piece to her mother, leading the conversation to a less emotional topic. She would not cry on the phone, especially on Christmas Day.

They talked for a few more minutes, and then Luciana wished her family a happy day, asking them to send hugs and kisses to everyone else. After hanging up, she got in the shower and let the sluicing water disguise the rest of her tears.

By the time she arrived in the kitchen, Jack and his mom and grandma were already there. Nonna was wrapping her knit projects, and Jack and Paola were elbow deep in dinner preparations.

"Merry Christmas," Luciana said.

"Ah, *Luchana*," Nonna said.

She kissed the ladies on the cheek, and when she got to Jack he gave her a half hug and kissed her temple. "More later," he whispered in her ear.

If his mom and grandma noticed, they didn't comment.

"How do you say *Merry Christmas* in Portuguese?" Paola asked.

"*Feliz Natal*," Luciana said. "I'm guessing Feliz is *Felice* in Italian and Natal is *Natale*."

"*Si*." Nonna smiled. "We usually say *Buon Natale* in Italy."

"Italian and Portuguese have a lot of similarities," Luciana said. "We also say *Bom Natal*."

Jack put down a plate with food and a glass of orange juice in front on Luciana. "I know you don't like a big breakfast, so it's only a small portion."

"What is it?" she asked.

"Our traditional Christmas morning breakfast called *strata*," Jack replied. "I didn't make as much today since it's only us for breakfast, but I know Kate and Leah will want some later."

Luciana took a bite. "This is delicious. What's in it?"

"It's a savory bread pudding with pork sausage, cheese, and herbs," Jack said.

She thanked him, and he went back to the meal preparations. Nonna finished her wrapping and moved the gifts to under the Christmas tree.

"Did you talk to your family yet?" Paola asked.

"My mom called and I talked to her and my Dad and brothers. She was worried I'd be alone today, but I told her I'm spending Christmas with the most awesome family." Luciana stood and took her plate to the sink. "I want to thank you again for inviting me," she said.

Nonna embraced Luciana. "We're the lucky ones," she said with a big smile.

"What Mamma said," Paola added. "We're so glad you can spend the holidays with us, aren't we Jack?"

Luciana and the DiLorenzo women paused to look at Jack. He turned to look at each one of them, then smiled wide at Luciana. "Absolutely."

The warmth in his eyes set her heart pounding in her chest. Maybe she wasn't spending Christmas with her family, but she had the next best thing—a family who'd taken her in, and a man who'd be easy to fall in love with.

However surprising the thought was, it was true none-theless, and she was at risk of losing her heart to Jack.

Luciana spent the rest of the afternoon helping Jack and Paola get ready for dinner and for the arrival of the family. When she heard Paola and Jack discussing sleeping arrangements, she offered to give up her bed.

"What if I sleep on the couch? Will that help?" Luciana asked.

"Sorry, I'm calling dibs on the couch," Jack said with a smile.

Paola shook her head. "What he means to say is that we have enough beds. Kate and her husband will be in my room, I'll be sharing Mamma's bed, Jack is taking the couch, and Leah and her husband and the baby will be in Jack's bedroom."

"What about the kids?" Luciana asked. According to what they'd told her, there were six kids and a baby.

"They all bunk in the attic," Paola said. "They love it. All the cousins together. Even the older ones."

Luciana frowned. "In the attic? Doesn't it get too cold up there?"

Paola turned to the linen closet in the hallway and pulled out a stack of sheets. "Jack, why don't you take Luciana to see the attic, and you two can make the beds?"

Jack grabbed the sheets from his mom and smiled at Luciana. "Follow me."

She followed him up the stairs to the second floor. At the end of the hallway, Jack opened a door that led to a second set of stairs. At the top they came to a wide room with two sets of bunk beds, one on each side. Windows at each end of the room and two skylights strategically placed let plenty of light in.

"This is a really cool room," Luciana said.

"It was my favorite when I was a kid," Jack said.

He put down the sheets on the carpeted floor and grabbed the mattresses from each of the top bunks. In a few minutes, he and Luciana had placed the fitted sheets on each mattress. Then he pulled out from under the bottom bed to reveal one more.

"Trundle beds," he said. "A place to sleep for everyone."

"What about flat sheets?"

"They bring their own sleeping bags. It's part of the experience at Grandma DiLorenzo and Nonna's."

Luciana looked around. "If my brothers and I and our cousins had such a room this far from the adults, we never would have slept." It had been bad enough with the lot of them spread over two or three bedrooms when they got together.

Jack chuckled. "Yeah, there's a lot of that going on. But the door stays open always, and I come and check on them."

"To play with them, I bet," Luciana said.

This time Jack laughed. "Don't tell my sisters. They don't know."

"Of course they know. They're mothers, and mothers know everything. Most likely they don't want to get out of bed so they let you deal with their kids instead."

Jack approached Luciana. "You're going to tell on me, aren't you?" His voice was playful, and his eyes shone with amusement.

"I wouldn't dare," she said.

When he looped an arm around her waist, the playfulness turned into something more intense and intimate. Jack leaned in, parted her hair away from her neck, and kissed her in the spot below her ear.

"I've been dying to do this all day," he murmured.

Luciana closed her eyes and grabbed on to his arms.

"Jack. Luciana." Paola's voice came from the bottom of the stairs. "Are you done up there?"

Jack took a small step back, but kept his hands on her waist. "We just barely started," he whispered, then shook his head. "Yep, we're done," he said, turning his face in the direction of the stairs.

"I think Leah's here," his mom said from the same spot.

"Coming," Jack replied to Paola. He took a breath, then touched his forehead to hers. "There goes all the privacy."

Luciana chuckled. "I didn't know you could be so dramatic." She gave him a peck on the lips and hurried out of the attic room. "Come on, let's go see who's here."

She was looking forward to meeting the rest of Jack's family.

Monday, December 25th ~ evening

From his spot on the kitchen island, Jack looked around the living room, and a slow smile formed on his lips. Amy and her family would be coming for New Year's Eve, but Kate had arrived soon after Leah, despite the road conditions. The craziness had officially started. Four extra adults and seven children in the house certainly made for a special day.

Dinner had been served at five, and, after cleaning up the table to set up the desserts, everyone had congregated around the Christmas tree to open the extended family presents and play games. The children took turns between the game-playing and the gift-opening, while their parents tried to keep them from getting overly excited. Luciana sat in one of the stuffed chairs reading a Christmas book to two of his nieces, both four and only three months apart. Sometimes cousins were as close as siblings.

Watching the two couples—Kate with her husband, Ryan, and Leah with Kyle—as they laughed and sat together and shared inside looks and specials moments, had Jack wishing he could have that kind of closeness with someone else. The feeling was one he'd almost forgotten—two years ago he'd been numb and shocked at Madison's departure, and last year he'd barely participated in any of the Christmas festivities. His holiday depression had been strong enough to warrant medicine. He still had the occasional bad day, but since he'd met Luciana he couldn't remember having one.

As if sensing him looking at her, she lifted her eyes to him and smiled. Maeve, one of his nieces, pulled at Luciana's arm and pointed at the book, and Luciana resumed the reading.

Throughout most of the day, Luciana hadn't strayed too far, working alongside him comfortably, or playing with the children who'd taken an interest in her. At times, Luciana caught him watching her, and they'd exchange a smile and a look, as they had just now, and it left Jack wishing he could take her in his arms and kiss her. Just the suggestion of a kiss sent his pulse soaring.

It was useless denying it—he was falling in love with Luciana.

How had his stunted, frozen heart fallen for a woman who didn't even live in this country? She was the one who'd melted the ice block in his chest, who'd made him believe in love again, who'd given him the courage to put aside his fears and want to take a leap of faith. He wanted happiness with Luciana and no one else.

What would happen when she left this week? Her life was in Portugal, where she had her family and her work, the career she'd built for herself. What was Jack going to do to keep himself in her life? She was his first thought every morning and his last every evening, and he couldn't go to the way he was before she'd entered his life—he didn't want to.

Nonna came and sat at the nearby table on the chair closest to him. "It's good to see you happy, *ragazzo*."

"I am happy." He couldn't fool Nonna, even if he wanted.

"But you also have worry," she said.

Jack nodded slowly. "I do. She's leaving soon."

"And she lives very far away. I understand." Nonna raised her finger at him. "You need to understand that love has no ... *frontiere. Come se dice?*"

"Frontiers? Boundaries?" Jack offered.

"*Si*. Love has no boundaries of country or time. I marry your nonno and we come to America right away. No family, no friends. He work all day, I work all day. Very lonely." She paused for a moment, as if remembering those days. "But I come with him

166

because I know our love was true."

"You're saying I should follow Luciana to Portugal?"

She shrugged. "No. I only tell you what I did. You decide what you do. You decide if the love is good for a fight."

She stood from the table and kissed him on the cheek. "Me and your mamma, we see something in that girl when she come for the first time. Now you do what is best."

Nonna walked to the sofa, leaving Jack there to think about what she'd said. Her words had been plain, even if the English was less so—she'd meant Jack had to decide if the love he had for Luciana was worth fighting for.

But what if Luciana didn't feel the same way for him? How would he find the courage to risk his heart again?

Later, after the children were tucked in their beds, and the adults retired to their bedrooms, Jack sat on the sofa in the living room and sent Luciana a text.

Are you still up?

Knitting a little project, came her reply.

Come knit down here.

Coming.

She appeared with a small canvas bag in her hand and took a seat next to him. "Where's everyone?" she asked.

"It took a few tries, but the kids are finally out. I checked to make sure. Their parents claimed to be too tired and went to bed too."

Luciana glanced at the clock. "It's already after ten thirty. A little later than I thought."

"It was a long day too." Jack scooted closer to Luciana and brought his arm around her shoulders.

Luciana turned to him. "You have seen Nonna knit, right?"

Jack smiled, pleased to hear Luciana refer to his grandma the same way he did. "Plenty of times," he replied.

"So you know a knitter needs lots of elbow room?" She looked down at their arms pressed together, then brought her eyes back to him.

Jack smiled, guessing what she implied. "This is when I should probably confess I didn't ask you to come down here to knit."

"Honesty is good," Luciana said, her eyes locked on him. "What do you have in mind I do then?"

Jack reached for her hand with his free one. "Maybe we can talk?" If only he could have more time to get to know Luciana. "How did your Christmas Day go? I noticed you looked a bit emotional when you came down for breakfast." He hoped she wouldn't think he was prying.

"Talking to my family made me homesick," she replied. "Even though my parents and brothers live in Porto and I live in Lisbon, I always make the trip up north for the holidays where we go to my grandparents, and all the cousins get together."

"You miss them," Jack said.

"I do. I did," she corrected herself. "Spending Christmas with your family has been the best experience." Luciana leaned her head on his shoulder, and they settled more comfortably against each other. She played with his fingers almost absentmindedly, as if they did it often.

Everything with Luciana was new, with a hint of familiar in his heart, like they'd known each other before and were finally reunited now.

"I took this job to avoid my cousins' wedding planning, and what I got in return went beyond any expectations I ever dreamed." Luciana lifted her head and looked at him. "Especially you."

Jack kissed her, unable to find the words to respond. His arm tightened around her back, and his other hand slipped to the back of her head as the kiss deepened. A thrill of emotion surged in his chest and radiated in a wave of heat.

How could he let Luciana leave without letting her know how he felt about her?

CHAPTER THIRTEEN

WEDNESDAY, DECEMBER 27TH

The snow stopped late on Christmas Day.

Early yesterday morning, Jack took Luciana back to the inn and an hour later she returned to work at the museum.

The weather center reported a total of thirty inches of snow, which was almost seventy-six centimeters, and Luciana could hardly believe the piles of snow that had been shoveled to the side of the streets and sidewalks. How messy would it get when it started melting?

Paola had insisted Luciana borrow the insulated coat and snow boots, and Luciana promised to return the items before she left. She'd have no use for them in Lisbon. Until she traveled back home, Luciana walked to the museum in the morning, and Jack picked her up in the evening to have dinner at his home. How quickly new habits formed.

Luciana's work at the museum was a day and a half behind schedule, and she started an hour earlier and stayed an hour later on Tuesday, trying to catch up. By midday on Wednesday, the snow returned, this time heavier and fiercer than before. Within the hour, she received an email from the airline informing her the flight to Lisbon had been canceled.

As the weather conditions worsened, Augustus Wynthrop sent everyone home and closed the museum, and when Luciana texted Jack with the news, he showed up to get her in ten minutes. This time she was already packed since she'd checked out of the inn earlier that morning.

Paola and Nonna hugged Luciana when she came in the door.

"*Luchana*, you are back," Nonna said with a big smile.

"Can you believe they closed the airports?" Luciana said to the ladies. "Looks like I'm stuck with you again."

"I'm taking your suitcase up to your bedroom," Jack said as he climbed the stairs.

She smiled. Her bedroom, as if she had a regular spot with the DiLorenzos. "Thanks, Jack," she said.

Luciana hung her coat and put away the boots to dry, grabbed the slippers from the closet, then followed Paola and Nonna to the kitchen.

"Are you staying an extra day?" Paola asked.

"I'm staying until the airport reopens, if that's okay with you," Luciana replied. "My room reservation at the River View Inn ended today, and Mrs. Wells is bursting at the seams with skiers."

"Of course it's okay. Nobody's using the bedroom and the house is back to being quiet after Kate and Leah and their families left. Amy and her family will be here on Saturday to spend New Year's Eve with us. We won't be half as crowded as before, so don't worry about space."

"As long as you're sure. I don't want to be the guest that overextends her stay. If I find any upside-down brooms behind your front door, then I'll know." Luciana chuckled at her joke, but the ladies remained impassive.

"What does the upside-down broom mean?" Paola asked.

"It's just an old Portuguese joke, like a solution to get unwanted guests moving on." Luciana's cheeks heated. "Sorry. I guess cultural jokes are not good to use when other cultures don't have the same traditions."

Paola waved a hand. "Don't worry about it. We have plenty of those customs in Italy too."

Since spending time with the DiLorenzos, Luciana had become aware of the similarities between Portugal and Italy. In some ways, the two cultures were closer than what Portugal had in common with the neighboring Spain.

"We had minestrone soup for lunch. Would you like some?" Paola asked.

"That would be great, thank you," Luciana replied. "I left early this morning and worked through the lunch hour trying to get as much work done as I could, and I just realized how hungry I am." Her stomach rumbled, and she covered it with her hand. "And there you have the sound effects to prove my statement."

Paola chuckled and placed a bowl of steaming soup and a sliced loaf of bread in front of Luciana.

"It smells divine," Luciana said. "Both the soup and bread."

"Jack make it," Nonna said and settled on her chair with a different project in her needles.

"Do you mean he made the bread?" Luciana asked in between bites.

"And the soup," said Paola. "He was restless this morning; woke up even earlier than normal."

"Because you leave today," Nonna said.

"Mamma," Paola replied to her mother's statement with a raised eyebrow.

"I was planning to come after work and say goodbye," Luciana said. "But I didn't leave. I'm here again."

Nonna and Paola exchanged a knowing look and resumed their tasks, leaving Luciana to wonder what they thought about her being back.

Had Jack thought Luciana hadn't planned to come by before she left?

Their time together on Tuesday evening had been charged with unasked questions and a latent tension. How could she say goodbye to Jack?

But thanks to another snowstorm, she wasn't leaving yet. Not today and probably not tomorrow.

Luciana washed her dishes, then excused herself to call her family and break the news she wouldn't be back in the morning. As long as she made it back to Catarina's wedding on January first, she would put the worry aside and enjoy her time with the DiLorenzo family.

In the early afternoon, while Nonna took a nap and Paola closed the café, Luciana retrieved her bag of works-in-progress to continue on the hat she was knitting for Jack. He was out delivering bread and clearing steps and porches around the neighborhood, which made this the perfect time for Luciana to knit without being interrupted.

The wool blend she'd bought at The Knotty Knitters was of superb quality. Luciana had noticed Jack didn't have a hat to wear under the hood of his coat, which made the perfect gift to give him. Something she made herself.

She'd knitted scarves, hats, and even sweaters for family members and friends, but she'd never knit an item for a man she cared for.

She cared for Jack. She actually liked him a lot and knew she could easily fall in love with him, if she wasn't already there. Knitting the hat for him was giving him a part of her that was tangible, something that would warm him physically, and maybe even remind him of her.

When the back door clicked, and the sound of steps reached Luciana, she put the knitting away and rose to meet Jack. She found him in the laundry room, standing on the rug and shaking himself of the snow clinging to his outer clothes.

"You must be freezing," Luciana said.

He hung up his coat and slipped off his boots, one at a time. "Not too bad," he replied. "Nothing a hot shower won't cure." He removed his snow pants next and hung them to dry as well.

He removed his flannel shirt and stood there, in sweatpants and a thermal long sleeve top, smiling at her. "I was going to hug you, but I need to shower first. Can I ask you to wait a few minutes?"

"Take your time. I'll be here."

After Jack was gone, Luciana walked to kitchen to warm up soup for him. The words she'd said to him lingered—*I'll be here*.

Such three simple words with so much meaning.

But she wouldn't be here for much longer.

FRIDAY, DECEMBER 29TH

Jack had been waiting all morning for Luciana. She'd gone to the museum to finish the project and to say goodbye to everyone there. She said she'd come to the café by lunchtime, but, of course, his patience was wavering. He wanted to see her—it was as simple as that. If someone had told him how quickly and deeply he'd become attached to a woman in only nineteen days, he would have laughed in their face.

But here he was, looking up to the door every time it swung open.

It didn't help his anxiety that she was supposed to find out when she could return to Portugal. It had stopped snowing last night, and, despite the airport reopening after a thirty-hour shutdown, it was still quite crowded and chaotic.

When Luciana entered through the side door to the café's kitchen, Jack turned from the counter to look at her. "What's the update?"

She unwound her scarf and unbuttoned her coat, then pulled out a chair and sat down on the other side of the counter. "I got a message saying to call a phone number for the airline, and I talked to a customer service agent. The airport is open but there's a waiting line for the flights and a wait list for the passengers in each flight."

A twinge of concern pricked Jack's chest. "When are you leaving?"

She gave him a small smile. "On Sunday afternoon."

Relief coursed through him. "We have some time then." She wasn't leaving just yet. His mind raced to plan something for the afternoon. "I have to work until after lunch, but can we spend some time together later?"

"Of course," she said. "I'm going to call my family and see what else I need to do to get ready."

She stood and grabbed his hand until they were out of sight from the customers in the café, went on tiptoes, and kissed him.

Jack thread his hands in her hair and neck, but she stepped away. "That was not a kiss," he complained.

Luciana chuckled. "You have panini to make, and I have things to do. I'll see you after lunch?"

"Definitely," he said.

As soon as Luciana left, Jack called Liam and asked him if he could work for one hour after lunch and help Mom with the closing, to which Liam said yes. With that plan in place, Jack turned ideas in his mind for his date with Luciana while he took orders from the customers who'd dared out of the house with so much snow still on the ground.

Two hours later, he drove the truck up the mountain with Luciana sitting next to him in the passenger seat.

"Are we going to the resort?" she asked.

"Yes, but I promise no skiing and no chair lifts." He glanced at her and smiled. "We're doing something different."

The roads had been cleared in anticipation of the New Year's Eve crowds, and Jack was glad the place wasn't as full today as it would be by Sunday.

After finding a parking place, they exited the truck and Luciana tucked her hand in the crook of his elbow. "Can you tell me what we're going to do?"

"We're going ice-skating," Jack said. "But if you'd rather not, we can find something else to do. To me, it's more important that we spend time together and less important what we do."

"With that kind of reply, how can I say no?" Luciana said with a smile. "I'll give it a try."

After renting the ice skates and helmets, Jack led Luciana to the outdoor rink where several families already skated. Mounds of snow had been plowed to the sides, and, despite the low temperatures, everyone looked to be at-ease and having fun. They sat on a bench and Jack helped Luciana into her skates, then put his on and his helmet, and tucked their boots out of sight, while she placed her helmet on her head.

He stood and extended his hand to help Luciana.

Once on her feet, she wobbled and clung to the railing on the side. "I'm not so sure about this," she said.

"Go easy and slowly until you get used to the feeling of standing on ice," Jack told her. "It also helps to keep your knees bent and to keep lower to the ground." He showed her the positions.

Luciana hung on to the railing for a few minutes, looking insecure.

"Put your arms out, and march in place carefully." Jack continued giving her tips.

"Did you look up ice-skating for dummies or something?" she asked, following his instructions.

Jack chuckled. "No, but I watched a video on 'how to learn to skate in three minutes,'" he confessed. "It's been so long since I learned. I wanted to make sure I could help you."

Luciana glanced at him from her position, her arms out and her knees bent a little too much. "You're always so thoughtful, Jack."

Jack stuck to her side, in case she needed help. "I feel guilty for the fall you took when we went skiing."

"It was not your fault. I should have paid more attention."

She hadn't moved much from her spot.

"Ready to try a few steps?" Again, Jack took his time and showed Luciana how to propel herself on the ice.

After a few minutes, her confidence grew, and she started taking longer strides. "I think I'm getting the hang of this," she said with a smile. "Maybe I can do a winter sport after all."

Jack's chest warmed at seeing Luciana content and having fun. He couldn't stop grinning. Every time they spent time together, the connection he felt toward her deepened, and he was beginning to be in denial about her departure.

Half an hour later, they returned the skates and poles and Jack took Luciana to the main lodge where the restaurant was located.

"This place is amazing," Luciana said as she looked to the cathedral ceiling. "Are those chandeliers made of deer horns?"

"Not real ones," Jack replied. "They're just made to look like that."

Luciana removed her hat and coat. "I feel under-dressed for the occasion."

"It's a ski lodge. They're used to guests in winter clothes and ski gear."

They followed the maître d' to a secluded table by a large window, and, after Luciana sat down, Jack took the chair closest to her instead of sitting across. In the fading day outside, the Christmas lights at the resort twinkled merrily, adding the perfect touch to the view.

After ordering their dinner, Jack pulled out a piece of paper from his pocket. "I hope you don't think this is weird, but I printed out some questions." He swallowed, suddenly more nervous than he'd anticipated.

"What kind of questions?" Luciana asked.

"Questions we can ask to help us get to know each other better," Jack said. "We don't have to do it if you don't want to."

"I love the idea," she said. "Go ahead and ask the first question."

Jack unfolded the sheet of paper and smoothed out the wrinkles. "What was the last book you read without skipping through anything?"

She chuckled. "At the risk of sounding like I only care about knitting, it was *A History of Knitting Around the World,*" she said, explaining what she liked about the book.

Throughout the rest of dinner, they took turns asking each other the questions Jack had brought, sometimes sharing related experiences and other times veering into different topics. The conversation flowed naturally between them as they learned more about each other.

While they waited for dessert, Luciana leaned toward Jack and looped her arm through his. "Thank you, Jack. This has been the best day."

Her voice was intimate and her eyes warm, and Jack wished he could make this moment last for longer than one night.

"It's you," Jack said. "You make everything better."

CHAPTER FOURTEEN

*A*my and her family arrived just before lunch.

Jack was glad they'd made the trip, and after a family meal, he played board games with his nephews and niece, and Luciana. The atmosphere in the home was charged. Even though they were not as loud as Kate and Leah's families, with a twelve-year-old, a ten-year-old and an eight-year-old, peace and quiet were harder to come by.

As much as Jack wanted to spend the day with Luciana, with a house full of people and children, it was nearly impossible to have a moment— let alone an entire day with her.

Sometime in the late afternoon, Jack found her in the laundry room, sitting on the floor with legs crossed on a pile of blankets, listening to a music list on her phone. He sat beside her, and Luciana pulled out the ear buds.

"I'm just doing a last batch of washing and drying before I zip my suitcase," she said.

"Nice spot." He smiled. "With the door closed, and the machines going, you can hardly hear anything else."

"Was this your mom's refuge when you were growing up? I bet you were a handful," she said with a teasing smile.

"Not even. Kate and Leah got in more trouble than I ever did," Jack said. His younger sisters were close in age and had been quite fond of making mischief.

"I'll have to check with your mom," Luciana said. "She might remember things differently."

Jack laughed. "I wouldn't be surprised."

She elbowed him playfully. "I'll be out in a few minutes."

Jack reached for her hand. "Not yet. I've been trying to find you alone all day." He pulled her to his side in a soft embrace and kissed her brow. "I missed you."

Luciana placed her hand over his heart. She leaned up and kissed him lightly on the lips.

Jack's mouth curved into a smile. "You missed me too."

"Maybe a little bit," she teased.

Jack reached for his pocket and took out his cell phone. Hesitation filled him for a moment. He'd been debating for days what to do when Luciana left. The time when Mom and Nonna had conspired to set him up with Luciana came to his mind—back then, he'd been relieved to find out she was only staying for two weeks. Thanks to the storm, she'd stayed a few more days, but just over two weeks with Luciana were not enough. He was beginning to feel lost.

"I want to stay in contact." He tapped on the screen. "Is that okay with you?"

Luciana took a deep breath, and the conflict flashed in her eyes before her expression relaxed. "Yes, I'd like that."

She'd been debating what to say; he'd seen it. What had made her change her mind? Maybe it was better he didn't know. For now it was enough that she agreed to let him stay in touch with her. Unless she kept the international plan she had here in New York, the texting wouldn't work, but at least he'd be able to video chat, send messages, or do some other kind of communication. As long as he didn't lose track of her, he didn't care which way it was.

Luciana turned sideways and laid her head on his shoulder. Jack lifted his arm around her shoulders and brought her closer to his side. He picked up his phone and extended his arm in front of their embraced shape while she smoothed her hair, tucking it behind her ears. He put a finger on the screen and took the picture. When it was done, he lingered a kiss on her forehead and pressed down again.

Two pictures to sum up her two weeks in Hudson Springs. It wasn't enough.

Jack scrolled back to the pictures and nodded in satisfaction. The lighting was less than ideal, and the floor of the laundry room wasn't the best place, but he wished to have more pictures together, and he wasn't about to let her leave without a tangible record of her time here.

"Can I have a copy of those, please?"

Jack texted them to her. "What are your plans when you get home?" he asked, eager to keep her talking, to know more of her life in Lisbon.

"I have to drive from Lisbon to the country. My cousin Catarina is having her daughter's christening on Monday morning and getting married in the evening."

Jack raised an eyebrow. "Shouldn't it be the wedding first then the christening?"

"It's not like that." She swatted at his arm. "She lost her first husband earlier this year, then found out she was pregnant, then she went away to our cousin Filipe's country house where she met the man she's getting married to." She sighed. "Their story is so romantic."

She told him about her family and who'd be there and how much she was looking forward to seeing everyone. Jack laced his fingers through hers and listened, acutely aware he wouldn't be a part of her days anymore, wishing for something he knew he couldn't have.

This was how he wanted to remember his time with Luciana—just the two of them together, even if it was on the floor of the laundry room.

Luciana looked around the front room of the DiLorenzos one last time. She'd said goodbye to Paola and Nonna in the morning, thanking them for the hospitality she'd never be able to repay, and she'd exchanged addresses with them, promising to write. They and the rest of the family had gone to mass across town, now that the streets were cleared.

With everyone gone, the house was strangely quiet. The Christmas decorations were still up, the string lights still on. The sideboard was set with desserts and drinks for the New Year's Eve celebration tonight, another custom that was like the Portuguese one. By then, she'd be on a plane headed to Lisbon.

When she turned, Jack stood at the bottom of the stairs, hands in his pockets and head down. "Will you let me drive you to the airport?"

She shook her head. They'd talked about it already—Jack wanted to prolong their time together, and she didn't. It wouldn't help at all; it would only make it harder. "Frank Callaway is picking me up."

Matt Garrison had arranged the ride, as Jack knew. She'd be leaving Hudson Springs the same way she'd arrived from the airport, in a private car. So much had happened during her time here.

Before the chance was gone, Luciana removed the small package from her purse. "I wasn't sure I'd be able to finish this in time, but I was." She handed it to Jack.

"Can I open it now?"

She nodded, and Jack quickly unwrapped the paper, turning the item in his hands.

"It's a knit cap," she said. "I noticed you don't have one." She'd estimated the head circumference, not wanting to give away the surprise, and she hoped it would fit.

"It's amazing," Jack said in a low tone. He put it on and turned to the mirror in the entry hall. "It fits great." He pulled it off. "What's it made of? The softness is incredible."

"It's a blend of merino, cashmere, and yak wool." The dusky blue color complemented Jack as she'd thought it would. The yarn was a luxury, one of the softest blends she'd ever worked with, and she'd knit the cap in a simple two/two rib with cables that graduated into a fitted crown.

The corner of his mouth rose in a crooked smile. "Yak wool? Is that even a thing?"

She chuckled. "You'd be surprised what can be spun into yarn."

He fingered it again. "It's amazing," he repeated. "You're amazing. Thank you." He stepped forward and kissed her on the cheek in a very simple gesture.

Luciana closed her eyes in a last effort to memorize the feeling of Jack close to her. If only there was a way of keeping the memories intact. She wished she'd be able to remember his dark eyes, the deep voice, the honest smile, the way his hair curled around his ears, his freshly baked bread scent, and the taste of his cinnamon kisses. If only she could knit her memories into a blanket with all the details that had made her time in American special. Even this brief moment.

A knock sounded at the door, and Jack opened it.

Frank greeted them. He grabbed her suitcase and the work carry-on sitting nearby. "I'll be in the car when you're ready, Miss Romano."

"Thanks, Frank," Luciana replied.

She stepped away from Jack and walked toward the front door, where Jack leaned against the wall. He followed behind her and took her hand.

Time to put on her brave face. "I guess this is it." A deep breath, then a smile. She blinked rapidly, hoping Jack didn't notice the unshed tears in her eyes.

His arms came around her, pulling her into a tight embrace. "Luciana," he whispered.

She pressed her face to his chest and closed her eyes. "Jack." She pulled back to look at him. "Maybe we can give this a try," she told him.

His expression held a hint of frustration, maybe even confusion.

"You mean this between us?" he asked.

"Lots of people do long-distance."

Jack hesitated, and Luciana doubted herself. Was this what she wanted? A boyfriend across the ocean?

"Will you at least think about it?" she asked Jack.

"I will," he replied with a nod.

She would be thinking about nothing else.

One last hug, a slow and tender kiss laded with longing, and then he let go of her, taking a step back.

Luciana shouldered her purse and walked down to the car, where Frank opened the door to let her inside the vehicle.

As Frank pulled away from the curb, she turned to look at the DiLorenzo house. Jack stood on the porch. He brought his fingers to his mouth and blew her a kiss.

When would she get a chance to see him again?

CHAPTER FIFTEEN

$\mathcal{L}$uciana held the baby to her shoulder as she bounced gently on the tips of her toes. From the corner in the corridor near the music room at Sunset Manor, she had a clear view to the entry hall and staircase. Chairs decorated with light blue covers and ribbons had been arranged in a semi-circular pattern facing the steps, and swaths of blue organdy wound through the banister. Afonso had recorded himself playing over the course of two weeks and the soft piano music played from concealed speakers, adding to the relaxed, warm ambiance in the manor house.

The dining room had also been dressed in light blues and shimmery pieces for a dinner following the ceremony. Even though not all the Romanos had been able to come, the house was full—full of laughter, full of family, and mostly full of love.

191

Following Carlota's christening in the Sete Fontes church, Tia Celestina and Tia Mariana, along with Avó Teresa, had put the final touches on the meal for after the ceremony.

No detail had been left to chance, and Luciana was anxious to see the bride walking down the aisle. And to think Catarina had protested, saying she didn't need a fancy party, but the Romanos knew how to throw a wedding, no matter the size. Thank goodness. Nobody deserved a happier, more beautiful day than Catarina and Afonso.

When a sudden hush came over the room, all heads turned upward. Catarina stood at the landing, the end of daylight filtering from behind her. She wore a vintage-inspired tea-length wedding dress in a barely-blue color and three-quarter sleeves with a sweetheart neckline. As beautiful as she looked, it was the radiance in her eyes and smile that stood out, and the way she gazed at Afonso.

Luciana looked at Afonso, and she held a breath. His expression.

Luciana's heart squeezed, and she nuzzled Carlota closer.

So much love, so much awe in Afonso's expression of gentle adoration.

That's what Luciana wanted. Someone to look at her with that much love in his eyes when he saw her.

Not just anyone—Jack DiLorenzo.

How many times had his eyes lit up when he saw her, and she hadn't recognized what it meant?

She sighed, and the baby startled in her sleep. Luciana shushed her softly while she watched Carlota's parents officially tie their lives together. She was happy for them, and, at the same time, couldn't help the twinge of longing that pinched her heart for a brief moment.

It was ridiculous to miss Jack so much. Less than forty hours since she'd said goodbye to the DiLorenzos, and already her chest ached with yearning.

How could she miss a man she barely knew? Three weeks was not enough to fall in love, was it? A memory flicked at her, a conversation at Catarina's baby shower. Hadn't Vanessa and Jacinta said something about falling in love in a short time? Maybe it was some sort of a Romano curse, to fall in love so quickly with someone from another country.

After Catarina and Afonso finished exchanging their vows, the officiator declared them formally married. Afonso wrapped Catarina in his arms, expertly dipped her in a graceful arc, and kissed her for a long minute. The room erupted in loud laughs and joyous clapping.

Luciana smiled and held the baby a little closer. "They made it, little one," she whispered softly. Emotion swelled in her chest, and she took a deep breath.

Later, as dinner was winding down, Luciana climbed the stairs to Catarina's suite, changed Carlota's diaper, and sat on the rocking chair to feed her a bottle. Outside the window, the night had fallen, darkness shrouding the landscape save for the flood-lights from the house.

Luciana rocked in the chair back and forth with the baby in her arms, enjoying the closeness and unwilling to put her down in her crib. The gentle, faded sounds of the family celebrating on the ground floor brought her a sense of contentment. She'd missed being around her family.

At the soft rustle of the door opening, Luciana turned to find Catarina entering the room. Catarina removed her shoes and approached silently on stockinged feet.

"Is the dinner over?" Luciana whispered, slowing the rocking, but not stopping. She put the empty bottle down on a nearby table.

Catarina nodded and knelt by the chair. "Has she been much work?" She asked in the same tone, looking down at the sleeping baby.

"None at all. She's a little angel." Luciana glanced at Carlota, unable to hold back the love she felt from her voice. "You know I love watching her." This time, the wistfulness tinged her words.

Catarina raised an eyebrow, but didn't comment. She stood and sat on the edge of the bed, poised as if she meant to stay for a little while. She opened her mouth, but Luciana spoke first.

"Isn't Afonso waiting for you?" Luciana asked.

"I came to get my long coat and luggage. We'll be leaving soon." She leaned forward, her expression softening again at the sight of her sleeping baby in

Luciana's arms. "And I had to see her one last time before I go."

Luciana offered a smile. "She's doing great."

Catarina raised her gaze to meet Luciana's. "What about you?" She asked in a low voice.

"What do you mean?" Luciana averted her cousin's inquisitive eyes.

"What happened in America, Luciana?"

Ah, that's what she meant. "I was never able to keep anything from you when we were young, was I?"

Catarina chuckled low. "Well?"

"I met someone," Luciana admitted. Slowly, she rose, walked the few steps to the crib, and lowered Carlota onto the mattress.

Catarina leaned closer. "I wanted to kiss her chubby cheeks, but if I touch her, she's going to wake up." She hesitated for a brief moment. "Be good to your godmother, *princesa*," she whispered, then blew a kiss to the baby.

Once the baby was settled and covered with a blanket, Luciana grabbed the monitor and stepped into the hallway, leaving the door ajar.

Catarina tiptoed to the side of the bed where a small suitcase rested on the wood floor and the long coat was draped over the footboard. She picked it up and followed after Luciana.

They stood outside the bedroom. "What's his name?" Catarina asked.

"Jack DiLorenzo," Luciana replied in a low voice. "Isn't Afonso waiting for you?" She repeated.

Catarina bit her lower lip and glanced toward the staircase. "When we return, you're going to tell me who Jack is and how you met him." She pulled on the handle of the suitcase and angled the wheels with a tap of her foot.

"I will," Luciana agreed. "But I'm warning you already, there isn't much to tell."

Catarina winked at her as she descended the stairs. "There's probably more than you think."

As Luciana joined the family at saying goodbye to the newlyweds in the entry hall, she turned her cousin's words in her mind.

Would she and Jack be able to figure out a way to have more between them? And how?

CHAPTER SIXTEEN

$\mathcal{L}$uciana spent the next few days snuggling Carlota and watching romantic comedies. By the time Catarina and Afonso returned from their three-day honeymoon on Wednesday morning, Luciana questioned the way she'd passed her time—holding the baby was wonderful, but witnessing fictitious characters get their happy ending wasn't as cathartic as she'd thought. Why couldn't real life be that easy?

The rest of the week was spent helping the newlyweds move into their townhome in Castelo Branco. Once again, Luciana took on baby duty, glad for the distraction and the busyness involving her cousin's little family.

When Luciana entered the kitchen on Friday, she found Catarina and Afonso at the table, Catarina sketching while Afonso fed the baby and watched the progress of the drawing. The sight of them was a beautiful, domestic vignette, one Luciana would miss, if not with a wish she could have the same.

"You're leaving?" Catarina stood and set aside the paper pad and pencil and stepped forward.

Afonso wiped Carlota's face, then picked her up from the high chair.

"Now that you guys are moved in and settled, it's time I return to Lisbon," Luciana said. "With the trip to New York and everything that happened there, plus the wedding, I haven't been home in almost a month. I'll need the time to reorganize before the next job comes along." In reality, she needed time to recoup and recharge from all the emotions.

Catarina frowned. "Do you have time for an early lunch before you leave?" She turned to Afonso.

Afonso adjusted the baby in his arms and tipped his chin toward the door. "Go. Carlota and I will keep busy." He winked. "Daddy-daughter stuff."

Catarina walked back and kissed them both. Then she turned down the hallway. "Let me get my coat and purse."

Twenty minutes later, Luciana and Catarina sat at a table by the window of the restaurant at the Dona Maria Hotel in downtown Castelo Branco. The afternoon was gray and cold, with a pale sun too weak to warm up the brittle January day.

As soon as the waiter took their orders, Catarina stretched her hand and touched Luciana on the forearm. "I'm sorry I've been so busy. We should have done this before, with more time. I didn't know you'd planned to leave before the weekend."

"You don't have to apologize. Getting you and Afonso settled in was more important."

"Are you sure I can't convince you to stay?"

Luciana shook her head. "It's time I go, before I get more smitten with my beautiful goddaughter." She would miss the baby fiercely.

The waiter came back with fresh cheese and butter and slices of toasted bread, and Catarina dug in. Luciana picked up a piece of bread and slowly spread a pat of butter on it.

"So. Jack DiLorenzo," Catarina said between bites. "How did you meet him?"

"The DiLorenzos have a bakery and café not too far from the museum where I worked. I went there for breakfast and lunch." She'd been there almost every day for the two-plus weeks she'd worked on the project. "When the snow storm came, Jack's mother and grandmother invited me to stay with them."

The waiter came with their food, and they busied themselves for the next few minutes.

"What happened?"

Luciana raised the glass to her mouth and drank, buying herself some time. How could she tell her cousin what she herself didn't quite know? She shrugged. "I spent three weeks in upstate New York. Not enough time for anything to happen."

Catarina frowned at her. "We have two cousins getting married soon who prove that theory to be wrong."

Luciana shook her head. "That doesn't mean—"

Catarina interrupted. "Jacinta and Knox fell in love in two weeks. And Matias and Vanessa had eight days on the cruise up the River Douro." She looked pointedly at Luciana. "It's more than enough time."

Luciana put down her fork and sighed. "Really, Catarina?" The weariness in her voice was too thick to disguise. "You really believe that falling in love in three weeks is not a little crazy? Even saying it out loud is making me sound like there's something wrong with me." She put her index finger to her temple and motioned the familiar gesture.

Catarina chewed for a moment, then took a sip. "Who can tell what binds two people together? For some the process is a little longer—" She placed a hand over her own chest—"and for others it takes less time. I don't think it means it's any less strong or undeserving. When there's a connection between two people, it's hard to argue with that."

Luciana looked out the window at the colorless, cold day. She missed the snow-capped rooftops and reds and golds of the lingering Christmas season in Hudson Springs. Tomorrow was January sixth and the first day of Epiphany, which meant the last day of lights and decorations. She would miss the closing of the season in the small town.

Despite the messages she'd exchanged with Jack, and one video chat, she missed him so much more than she thought she would. "Maybe there's some truth to that, but it doesn't matter. I'm here and he's there. Five thousand kilometers are hard to ignore." Before Catarina made any more comments on the subject, Luciana changed it. "You didn't tell me yet of your plans to open a decorating space."

Catarina raised an eyebrow, but in the end she conceded and swiped the screen on her smartphone. "Let me show you my Pinterest board."

When Luciana took Catarina back to the house, she followed her cousin inside to say goodbye to the baby and to Afonso.

Catarina stepped forward and embraced Luciana. "I'm so glad you were able to come. I'm going to miss you."

"I'll come back soon," Luciana promised. She returned the hug and exchanged air kisses with Catarina.

"Drive safe," Catarina said as Luciana opened the car door.

"Don't worry. I should be in Lisbon before dinnertime."

As Luciana pulled away from the curb, she sighed. She was looking forward to returning home, but after a month of being surrounded by family—Jack's family in Hudson Springs and her own for Catarina's wedding—the empty apartment would seem strange.

Maybe she'd get a cat. But what would she do with it when she had to leave on a work trip? What about a turtle? Turtles were easy pets, right? She could pay Senhora Marta's teenage daughter to watch over it when Luciana went out of town. But turtles didn't cuddle and purr and keep company to a lonely heart.

Was she so desperate for company as to seriously entertain the idea of taking in a pet?

Luciana shook her head, as if the gesture could bring some sense. Maybe if she kept busier than normal, she wouldn't have time to mope and feel sorry for herself, for feeling so incomplete.

She certainly wouldn't have time to spend any thoughts on Jack DiLorenzo.

Jack, with the deep, brown eyes and the soft, husky voice. The quiet smile she missed so much. The way he looked at her.

He'd asked her to let him know when she arrived at her apartment so they could video chat again. How was she going to keep a brave face?

CHAPTER SEVENTEEN

Luciana had been gone for a few days when Jack received her reply to his message. Every day he'd checked, reminding himself she needed the time and space to adjust back to her routine after being gone for several weeks, especially after her cousin's wedding. He wanted to call her on the phone but held back, knowing it would be harder to listen to her voice.

How did he miss her this much? Reopening the café after the short holiday break had been tougher than he could have predicted. He was distracted and imagined her sitting by the front window, sipping the caffé mocha and smiling at him. At home, it wasn't much better, where he could see her in almost every room, remembering the echoes of her voice and laughter, by the thread of memories that pulled at him unceasingly.

The time difference between New York and Lisbon was an inconvenience, even with the baker's hours he kept. It annoyed him that she lived ahead of him five hours, forcing him to a foiled game of catching up. A discreet routine inched up slowly, and Jack was relieved in the small predictions and daily expectations of knowing where and when to find her, following her comings and goings on social media. He messaged Luciana a few times a week, and she replied in short sentences. They'd had one video chat while she babysat her goddaughter, but Luciana had missed the second chat they'd set up, apologizing later. Talking to her and seeing her on the screen were the kind of slight consolations that lent him the balance he needed for now. Everything else chafed at him.

On Sunday before dinner, a week after Luciana had returned to Lisbon, Jack went for a drive. He circled the town square and drove past the museum, not sparing a second glance at the new sign announcing the textile exhibition. The one Luciana had restored, catalogued, and set up on display. More than three thousand miles separated him from Luciana, but there was a reminder of her time in Hudson Springs. A permanent reminder.

The Christmas lights were off, and tomorrow the decorations in town would come down, starting with the nativity scene, which would be dismantled and put away until December.

Memories could not be put away. He knew that only too well. At least this time they were bittersweet and not shame-ridden. The only thing he was guilty of was indecisiveness and fear. Fear of happiness and fear of losing.

Fear of loving again.

Jack drove on until he left town and kept driving south toward the city, running from everything that brought his heart wishing for things he'd told himself he couldn't have. He drove for hours, trying to make sense of everything in his life.

Mamma and Nonna were sitting in the living room when he returned. Jack removed his coat and scarf and hung them on the coatrack in the hallway. His hands lingered on the dark blue cap Luciana had knit for him before he placed it in the coat pocket.

"I kept your dinner in the microwave," his mother said.

He thanked her absently. He'd eat later.

Slipping his hands in his pockets, he walked to the French patio doors. Winter had a firm grip this season, and the plants on the patio showed no signs of life. In just a few months, the family would start the new seeds for the summer garden, as they did every spring.

"You dropped your cap," Mom said.

Jack turned around. "What?"

Mom gestured at the floor, and he walked back to pick it up.

She put the book down on the coffee table and joined him. "What do the instructions say for cleaning?"

"I have no idea." He handed her the cap. If he wore it every day during winter, he'd have to clean it at some point, but that was the least of his worries right now. Jack walked back to the French doors.

Mom pulled the cap inside out. "This is so well knit." She joined Nonna, who set aside her knitting. The two of them examined the cap almost reverently. "Weird," Mom said after a few minutes. "There's a tag but no care instructions. You should take a look at it."

"I will." Jack kept looking at the barren, snowy patio.

"Jack, you should look at it right now," she repeated in an even voice.

The comment annoyed him, and Jack tried to hide his impatience. Maybe he should have stayed out until Mom and Nonna were in bed. The thought brought a prickle of guilt and his shoulders dropped, more irritated at himself that anyone else. It wasn't his family's fault. "What's wrong with the tag?"

She returned the cap. "Nothing wrong. Just not what I was expecting. I'm guessing you haven't read it yet." Her teasing half-smile hinted at something, and his curiosity rose.

He'd noticed the small cream tag made of some kind of woven ribbon but hadn't really paid much more attention to it than that. Turning the lamp to cast the light his way, Jack flattened the tag against the knit fabric behind it. It was secured by a couple of stitches on both ends, and it had a printed row of small letters: *to-J-Handknit-by-L,* followed by the year.

Jack frowned. How had he missed this?

Maybe he should stop using it every day. It would wear out faster, and he wanted this cap to last forever.

"Did you see the other side?" Mom asked.

"What other side?"

"Turn it out. There's more inside."

Since the ribbon was only sewed on the ends, Jack turned it halfway toward him, then flipped the cap upside down to read: *With-All-My-Love*.

All. *My*. Love. Luciana's love.

Jack froze and held a breath. His eyes squeezed shut, and, for a moment, the sound of rushing blood drowned everything else around him. Could it be?

"Jack? Are you all right?" Mom asked.

He turned to them, the cap in his hand. "Yeah." He breathed out slowly. "Yeah, I'm all right. Excuse me, I gotta make some calls." He crossed the room to the staircase.

Mom met him at the bottom of the stairs. "Why? Are you going somewhere?"

Jack turned and nodded slowly, the warmth of a smile spreading from him. "I think I am."

Mom laced her fingers and smiled, then exchanged a look with Nonna, who'd paused her knitting to look at him. They grinned at each other, and Nonna said, "Alleluia."

His mother nodded. "It's about time."

It was about time. It had just taken him a while to figure it out. "I have to give it a try," he said to them.

"We know you do," Mom said.

"What about you two? And the café?" They'd been the focus of his life for so long.

"We be fine, Giacomo." Nonna called him by his childhood name. "The café be fine too. Your Mamma and I have a good plan. You need to worry about new things now."

"Go make your calls, and we'll tell you more about it," Mom added.

"What if it doesn't work out?" He finally voiced his fears, and relief followed.

His mother sighed. "Jack, we love you, but we can't tell you how to live your life." She gestured to her mother. "Your nonna and I agree with you; you have to give it a try. We support your decision."

Jack looked between them. "That's it then?" It couldn't be as simple as they made it sound, could it?

Nonna resumed her knitting, then glanced up at him without breaking her rhythm. "*Ragazzo mio*. More do. Less talk."

Mom kept smiling, and Jack chuckled. He walked over to where Nonna sat and kissed her head. "Always right, Nonna. Always right."

He repeated the kiss for his mom. "Wish me luck."

He was halfway up to his bedroom when he heard Nonna's yell. "*Buona fortuna.*"

The corner of his mouth rose in a half smile. His life had changed too much in less than a month. The kind of change he hadn't even gone looking for.

Two years ago, the woman he thought he loved had left with the first snow on what should have been the happiest day of his life. This time, a snowstorm had brought a woman he could easily love. A woman from Portugal he already loved.

How could he hide behind the excuse of three thousand miles?

MONDAY, JANUARY 15TH

Luciana looked out the window. It had been raining all weekend, and she'd used the weather as an excuse to stay in and start a new knitting project.

After helping Catarina and Afonso move into their townhouse, Luciana's family had asked her to come to Porto for a few days, but Luciana had effectively put them off, citing preparations for the new job at the Costume Museum, which didn't actually start for another week. A small detail she hadn't shared.

If she went to Porto, everyone would be expecting a report of her time in America, and what would she say? That she'd fallen in love with a man who might still be stuck in the past? It was easier to hide behind the pretense of being as busy and as happy as she'd always been.

She puttered around the apartment all day in her pajamas, looked at the Facebook page of the local animal shelter, and organized her knitting room. It only made sense to make her home office space more effective, especially if she was getting a turtle.

A message from Jack popped up on her phone. She closed her eyes and settled a hand over her chest. Deep breaths. Sometimes she didn't reply to him right away. Not to be rude, but to force herself not to call him.

How do I wash the cap you knitted for me?

She frowned. That was unexpected. **You need to wash it already?**

Yeah, but there's no instructions. Nonna said there should be a tag with washing instructions, but I can't find anything.

Luciana's heart sank. Something must have happened to the custom tag she'd stitched to the inside of the cap. No wonder he hadn't mentioned it. She'd put so much thought into it.

Cold water, mild soap, lay flat to dry, she typed back.

That's a bit too vague, came Jack's reply. **Are you home right now?**

Yes, I'm home.

Can we talk about it?

Talk about what? she asked him.

The washing instructions.

Luciana paused. As much as she wanted to talk to Jack, it would only hurt more in the long run. **It's pretty easy. I'll send you a YouTube link.**

I'd rather see you do it.

She didn't reply. What could she say to that?

The apartment bell rang and Luciana jumped. It was almost dinnertime and she wasn't expecting anyone.

She put the phone down and walked to the

210

intercom. "*Quem é?*"

When a soft knock sounded at the door, she stilled. Deep breath. She was off center after Jack's message and just needed to calm down. After a quick check on the mirror in the entry, she passed a hand through her hair, then flattened her palms on the door to look through the peephole.

A man in a dark blue cap.

Her heart tripped, and she stepped back with a hand over her chest.

No. How could it be?

Luciana unlocked the door and opened it. "Jack?"

He gave her a small smile. "Luciana."

That voice. Those eyes.

Her cheeks flamed, and her heart raced at the sight of Jack standing in front of her. She held on to the side of the door to keep her hands from shaking.

"Come in." She stepped aside to let him in.

Jack raised a hand to his head and slipped off the cap, holding it in his fingers. "I talked to Lily Kerrison at the yarn store," he said.

"The Knotty Knitters," Luciana added.

He nodded. "I asked her about the washing instructions, and she said, to be safe, I should ask the person who knitted it."

"You came all this way to ask me how to wash the cap?" She had so many questions. "What about the café? Your mom and Nonna? How long are you staying?"

"Momma and Nonna are fine, and the cousins

agreed to take more hours. The café is open from Tuesdays to Saturdays now, which helps keep the operations down until I get everything in place the way we need. For the time being, I hired an accountant to run the business part of things. He's someone I trust, an old friend from accounting school. I'm still looking for a full-time baker, but I'm confident someone will turn up to fill the position. Until then, I got a part-time baker filling in." His voice was confident, but his eyes held a hint of hesitancy.

"Why didn't you just call?" Her mind turned with everything she wanted to ask him.

He shrugged. "If I'd told you I was coming, maybe you'd tell me not to bother."

Would she have told him not to come? How many times had she thought of Jack coming to see her? Too many to count. And every time, she'd brought herself down from that wishful thinking, knowing it wouldn't work.

"I figured I had a better chance in person," he added.

"A better chance of what?"

"A better chance to know if you meant what you wrote on this tag." He turned the cap in his hands until the ribbon inside was exposed.

Luciana gasped. The tag was still there, and he'd seen it. Jack had read her message.

Jack stepped forward and took her hand, running a light caress over the back of it.

Her skin turned into gooseflesh, and Luciana closed

212

her eyes for a moment. "I meant it." She nodded slowly. Of course she meant it. "But—but I also have questions," she said with a sigh. She didn't want to question everything. "What about your mother and Nonna? You said you wouldn't leave them."

He frowned. "When did I say that?"

"When you told me about Madison. You said she knew you wouldn't leave your family." She remembered the words well.

"I wasn't ready to do that for her. But it's different now. You're not her, and I'm a different person too." Jack searched her eyes. "I don't have answers to all the questions, Luciana. I'm hoping you'll be willing to get those answers with me."

Luciana watched Jack closely. He lifted his free hand to touch her cheek, not breaking the eye contact.

Nervousness and vulnerability were there in his eyes. But so were hope and determination.

And maybe something more.

Luciana shortened the distance between them, and Jack's hand dropped to her waist, pulling her closer. She lifted her free hand and touched the side of his face. When his lips met hers, Luciana closed her eyes and clung to him.

All that she'd been missing since leaving Hudson Springs was restored to her.

She gave herself to the moment and didn't hold back.

Jack was here—holding her, kissing her—and she

finally felt complete. Nothing felt more right than this.

"I missed you so much," she said when they parted at last.

Jack touched her lips again. "I love you so much," he said in one breath.

Her eyes misted with unshed tears. "I love you too."

Jack's expression bloomed into a smile, and this time she leaned in, kissing him again.

Luciana sighed and pressed closer to Jack. "How are we going to make this work?"

"Together." He tightened his hold on her. "We can do it together."

EPILOGUE

THREE MONTHS LATER

$\mathcal{L}$uciana stood on the steps of the small church next to Catarina and Afonso, who held a busy Carlota in his arms.

The day was sunny and unseasonably warm, lending a late-June ambiance to what should have been a cool April day. Definitely better for a wedding.

When the church peals echoed from the tower, the smiling, happy couple exited through the front door. The family waiting for Jacinta and Knox on the steps erupted in loud cheers and clapping, some of them blowing bubbles from tiny white dispensers.

Jacinta wore a simple A-line dress and a lace veil that had been worn by her mother at her own wedding. Knox cut a dashing figure in a dark blue suit, his red hair contrasting next to his bride's dark brown. They stopped and waved at everyone, then he took her in his arms and kissed her soundly. The woots grew even louder. The photographer quickly assembled everyone for the group photos with the newlyweds.

"They look so happy," Catarina said.

Luciana nodded. "Two down, one to go." Matias and Vanessa's wedding was scheduled for mid-June.

"Two down, two to go," Catarina corrected with a knowing look.

Luciana shook her head. "If you mean me, that's not happening any time soon."

Catarina winked. "You never know what Jack has planned."

"What do you mean?"

"Shh, smile at the camera." Catarina looped her arm through Afonso's and held on to Carlota's hand.

Luciana turned to the front, but her mind raced. What did her cousin mean about Jack's plans? Did Catarina know something?

Jack and Luciana had been making the long-distance relationship work for the last three months while he settled the café with a new manager and new baker. She'd gone to visit Hudson Springs for a long weekend, and Jack had come to Lisbon once, but it had been almost three weeks since the last time she'd seen him in person. Video calls didn't make up for it. She hid a wistful sigh. No use getting mopey at Jacinta and Knox's wedding. They certainly deserved a happy day.

The couple kissed again before entering a black car decorated with white ribbons, and the rest of the family made their way to their own vehicles. The wedding guests would follow the bride and groom's car to the reception venue, honking the horns along the way, as was tradition.

Filipe approached Luciana. "Hey, little sis, do you need a ride?"

Their parents and younger brothers had already left. "Yes, thank you."

Catarina turned around. "I think I left Carlota's diaper bag inside the church."

Afonso had left to bring the car around, and Catarina's arms were full with the baby.

"I'll get it," Luciana offered.

The sound of her heels echoed inside the now-empty church. The sun streamed through a high window, casting rainbow light on the stone floor. For a moment, she almost wished she had the time to sit and think. The peaceful feeling called to her.

Luciana looked in the pew where they'd sat, but the bag wasn't there. After five minutes of looking and asking about it at the lost and found, Luciana exited the church to tell Catarina.

Everyone was gone. Catarina and Afonso's car had left, and so had Filipe's. They'd left her behind. She hadn't been gone that long, had she?

Luciana pulled out her phone to call for a taxi to take her to the venue. As she looked for the phone number, a black car with tinted windows pulled up to the sidewalk and stopped in front of her. Had someone sent a car for her after all?

The passenger side window rolled down. "I heard you need a ride," said a familiar voice.

"Jack?" She grinned. "When did you arrive?"

Before she had the time to open the door, he came around the car, and Luciana wound her arms around his neck.

Jack pulled her close and kissed her for a long minute. "Hmm. Feels like you missed me as much as I missed you," he said with a slow smile.

"You know I did," she whispered in his ear.

He tightened his embrace.

A passing car honked at them, and Luciana stepped back. Jack wore a dark gray suit and a light blue tie, one that precisely matched the color of the chiffon dress she wore. At the sight of him, her heart skipped a beat.

"If I'd known you'd look this good in a suit, I'd have asked you to wear one before," she said with another kiss.

"I couldn't show up to your cousin's wedding in chef's white, could I?" He gave her a crooked smile. "Sorry I missed the ceremony."

"We can still make it to the reception. They all left already. I was about to call a taxi—" Luciana stopped at the look in Jack's eyes. "They left me on purpose, didn't they?"

Jack opened the passenger side door and held it for her. "Come on, we better get going and join your family."

Luciana slid inside, and he closed the door behind her. Once he entered the car and sat behind the wheel, she leaned over and kissed his cheek. "I'm so glad you came. How long can you stay?"

Jack kissed her back, started the car, and merged into traffic. After a minute, he glanced at her. "Patience," he replied enigmatically.

Luciana nodded at Jack, making an effort to smile at him, and keep her expression pleasant.

They had an agreement between them—no matter how long or short one of them could stay for visits, the other would not complain or exude pressure.

But Luciana worried their future would be long coming, with him in New York and her in Lisbon. That he'd been able to come see her in Porto for Jacinta and Knox's wedding was a surprise, a very good one. She wouldn't say anything. Just having him here was enough. For now.

Still, the questions swirled in her mind. What did he want to talk about? Was this his last visit? Maybe it was time for her to think seriously about moving to the state of New York. She would miss her family, but she would miss Jack more if she could never see him again, and losing him was too high a price to pay. The prospect terrified her.

As deep as she was in her thoughts, she'd hardly noticed where Jack was going and was surprised to see they'd arrived at the hotel's parking lot. The restaurant was located on the second floor with a patio overlooking the river Douro and the Dom Luís Bridge, a place of significance for the bride and groom from a comment Jacinta had made before.

In the atrium, a poster in elegant script announced the Romano-Campbell wedding in the Bridge Room.

Luciana stepped toward the staircase, but Jack tugged at her hand.

"I thought I could wait to do this later, but I can't." A frown marred his forehead, and his eyes focused on a spot behind her.

Luciana's heart lurched. "Are you sure we can't wait? Everybody's upstairs and—"

He took hold of both her hands and shook his head. "It won't take long. I really need to do this now."

He looked both ways, then led her through a short hallway and opened a door to the outside, almost as if he'd been there before. They walked toward a small courtyard with a pergola covered in green foliage and purple blossoms, the heady perfume carried in the air by a light breeze. Jack indicated the iron bench tucked under, and Luciana sat down, relieved to see they were the only ones around. The momentary privacy was welcome.

"Jack, what's going on?" she asked.

Jack turned to her, tugging at the knot of his tie. He took a series of deep breaths and rolled his shoulders, as if trying to gather courage for the task.

Her chest squeezed at seeing him so nervous.

"I renewed my accounting license before it expired," he said. "Do you know accountants can work from anywhere? They only need a laptop and a good Internet connection."

"Does that mean you can stay for a while?" she asked, hopeful.

"In a way." He inhaled quickly, then took both of her hands and went down on one knee. "Luciana, will you marry me?"

A laugh bubbled out, even as big, fat tears rolled down her cheeks. "Yes. Of course I'll marry you." The happiness inside her threatened to burst, and she was anxious to show it. She moved her hands to Jack's shoulders and pulled him forward, landing her lips on his. He kissed her back.

Jack drew a ring from the right pocket of his suit jacket and slid it onto her finger. Rose gold, a small multi-faceted diamond in the center. Luciana didn't know anything about engagement rings, but this one looked vintage. "It's so beautiful," she whispered.

"It was Nonna's ring," Jack said.

He stood and took her in his arms, and she clasped her hands behind his neck.

"You've been so patient, waiting for me. I figured if we're to keep flying between Lisbon and New York, we'll do it as a married couple," he said.

It was the perfect solution, both of them having jobs that didn't require them to stay in one location. Luciana opened her mouth to tell him how much she agreed, but Jack kissed her and she soon forgot everything else.

All was right. They'd never be apart again.

Read Catarina and Afonso's story
in *Love Me At Sunset*.

CHAPTER ONE

$\mathcal{H}$ow much hope could a place hold for a new beginning?

Afonso arrived at the stone wall and dropped the canvas bag on the side of the road. The intricate monogram on each panel of the iron gate confirmed he was at the right place. Casa do Sol Poente—Sunset Manor. Was this his fresh start? A place named after his favorite time of day could only bring good luck.

In the valley below, the first shadows cast by the setting sun already inched closer to the foothills of the small village of Sete Fontes. The view opened far beyond the winding river to the red-roofed houses dotting the hills on the other bank.

He reached for his water bottle and took a long swig, appreciating the differences in the air around him. No traffic noises. No congested streets and crowded sidewalks. And more notably, no sounds of churning industrial-sized washers, the hiss of steam irons, and the always-present loud-cursing men he'd had to put up with during laundry duty.

Only the languorous clangs of the church bell and a couple of dogs barking at each other on a farm down the hill.

A slow smile pulled at the corners of his mouth. He liked it already.

The walk from the village had taken close to an hour, and he hadn't passed any other houses or farms in the last fifteen minutes. The promise of solitude bloomed more real than he'd thought possible.

Afonso swung the bag over his shoulder and placed the empty bottle in an outside pocket. The gate was ajar, and he passed through easily, noting the signs of neglect. The original color was hard to pick amid the rust stains, and it could use a good cleaning and a new coat of paint.

As he climbed the winding road past the bend, rows of hydrangea bushes lined the lichen-covered walls, the large blue petals brightening the old stones. Through the branches, a peek of stone caught Afonso's attention, but the thick foliage hid the rest of the house from view.

After the paved road curved sharply in the other direction, Afonso stopped. A woman stood at the edge of a weed-infested path, facing a row of mature linden trees. The golden light outlined her delicate figure, contrasting with the wildness of the bushes and vegetation behind her, a mass of twisted greens of various shades speckled with tiny buds of the red, pink, and yellow of a once-grand rose garden.

Before he had the chance to make his presence known, the woman clutched her middle and doubled over, retching violently.

Afonso turned away from her and took a step back, torn between the urge to help her and the need to give her privacy. Had she eaten something bad, or was she ill? His former training kicked in and his mind went through a list of possibilities.

After a few moments, she straightened and wiped her mouth with the back of her hand. She mumbled something and shook her head, the disgust in her tone clear and unmistakable.

Afonso shifted his bag. "Hey, are you okay?"

The woman shrieked and jumped back with a hand over her chest. When she turned to face him, her eyes widened with surprise, which was quickly replaced with something stronger. "This is private property," she yelled. "Who are you, and what are you doing here?" She flicked her eyes to the ground and her cheeks flamed red. "Are you some kind of pervert spying on people?"

Afonso shouldered his bag behind his back and raised his hands in a show of conciliation. "I'm sorry if I caught you at a bad moment. I promise I'm not spying on you." He spoke slowly, trying to diffuse the tension. "I'm here to meet with the owner."

She crossed her arms over her middle, and this time the disgust in her expression was surely directed at him. "He should be in the main house." Her tone was curt.

Afonso stepped back onto the private driveway and nodded a quick thanks to her.

Her eyes narrowed at him as she watched him go by. "You better not be lying."

He paused and met her eyes. "I don't lie." All the lies were in the past. He was done with that life.

She didn't reply, but her left eyebrow raised. In contradiction or skepticism, he couldn't tell.

When Afonso reached the clearing, he looked back, but she was gone. He gave himself a mental shake to push the strange encounter from his mind.

The manor house was large and almost as imposing as he'd expected. Its neoclassical style was reflected in the symmetrical lines of the windows on the ground floor and the row of Juliet balconies on the first floor. From the red-tiled roof, a pair of attic dormers rose on each side. A wide staircase led to the front where a heavy, paneled wooden door matched the green of the painted shutters. The effect was almost striking, minimized only by the intense disarray of all the vegetation surrounding the area. In its glory days, the granite house's grandeur must have been impressive.

Afonso climbed the steps. Even the door knocker was a classic. He lifted the iron hand holding a ball and smacked it against the metal plate on the wood surface.

After a few knocks, the door swung open.

A dark-haired man in his midthirties stood at the

entrance. "Hello. Can I help you?" His tone was friendly.

"I'm looking for Filipe Romano," Afonso said.

The man extended his hand. "I'm Filipe Romano." His grip was strong, and he made eye contact. "Are you Afonso Cortez by any chance?"

Afonso nodded. "I am."

Filipe Romano's expression relaxed into a smile. "Praise the heavens. I thought you'd changed your mind about coming. Please, come in."

The faint scent of new construction and aged wood permeated the air. The area was clean and void of furniture but for a large rug covering the aged marble floor in front of the stairs and a free-standing coat-rack made of heavy wood. The main staircase split in two at the first landing, one to each side of the house. The oval skylight let the sunshine in to spill naturally down the staircase, casting shadows into the corners.

Afonso took a moment to study Filipe Romano. He looked like a slightly older version of his cousin Matias, Afonso's former boss. The family resemblance was evident in the same brown eyes and high fore-head. "Sorry I'm late. The walk up was a bit longer than I thought."

"You walked from the village?"

"I'm without my own transportation at the moment." He was without a lot of things, a car being the least of those.

Filipe brought a hand to his chin as he gave Afonso an appraising look. "Well, I'm glad you made it." He gestured to the floor by the door. "Just leave your things there. I'll show you later where you can put them." He turned down the hallway to his right, and Afonso followed him to the first room.

"This is the music room. Well, it's an empty room now, but that's what the original design called for and I tried to preserve that."

In the corner, under a cover, the skeleton of a grand piano stood silent. Afonso turned away from it and flexed his fingers involuntarily.

Filipe glanced in the same direction. "That old piano came with the house, and I still don't know what to do it."

Afonso pretended he didn't either.

"I'm nearly done with the interior remodel." Filipe kept walking and gestured at the door opening as they passed from one room to the next without the connection of a hallway. "The kitchen and bathrooms are all done, and the interiors have all been painted. I'm trying to decide what to do about the decorating."

"Impressive work," Afonso said. The wood floors looked original as well, having been refinished to a polished gloss.

Filipe pushed the last door, and they entered a room that looked half-lived-in. A heavy mahogany desk sat by one of the windows, and a pair of wing-back chairs and a sofa in dark leather were positioned in front of the fireplace. The wall opposite the windows was lined with floor-to-ceiling shelves in the same mahogany, conspicuously void of books. From what he'd seen so far, even without furniture and decoration the mansion was grand.

"The books are in storage, and I didn't have the time to unpack them yet." Filipe gestured around. "So this is the office and library. In case you're wondering, the built-in shelves are original, but I had the desk made to match. Not exactly my taste but it goes with the house." He walked to the desk and cleared a pile of papers to the side. "The house sits square with the cardinal points and we still call this side the west wing." He unfurled a blueprint, tucked the corners under books, and set a solid glass paperweight on the surface.

Afonso approached and listened to Filipe's explanations of the house.

"For the time being, you'll be working in the areas immediately surrounding the house." Filipe tapped the paper again. "The road from the gate to the front door needs to be cleared. And the formal gardens require a lot of attention." He brought a smaller map from under the blueprint. "These are the original plans that I was able to unearth in Castelo Branco's register. There's an English-type garden with roses and boxwood hedges." He paused and looked up to Afonso. "You do have experience with yard work, don't you?"

"I have hands-on experience, but no formal training." All the summers Afonso had spent at his grandparents' working on the farm might finally pay off.

"That's good enough for me." Filipe turned back to the map, and Afonso followed along a series of geometric designs with numbers and a key written in a curled script on the margin.

Filipe slid a drawer open and drew out a tablet. "I hired a landscape designer who outlined each stage of the cleaning and restoration that needs to happen before the new plants come in." He pushed the tablet into Afonso's hands, and Afonso swiped the screen as he looked through the color-coded plans. "For now, I decided to start clearing the overgrowth and moving on with some of the smaller projects. It's all there on the tablet. Of course, you can always call me or send me a text if you have any questions," Filipe said.

Afonso raised his head from the screen. He must have missed something. Why would he need to call Filipe? "Won't you be here every day?"

Filipe sat on the sofa and indicated the chair to Afonso. "My plans changed. I'm in the middle of acquiring a property by the coast, and I need to be there. As much as I'd like to supervise the garden's restoration, it's not as pressing as the other project is. That's why I need a person I can trust to stay here."

Afonso returned the tablet to Filipe. "You do know where I've just come from, don't you?" What exactly had Matias Romano told his cousin about Afonso? As much as Afonso wanted this job, if Filipe wasn't aware of his past, he would quickly take back his offer.

"If you're referring to your recent release from prison, yes, I am aware of that." He leaned back

230

and crossed an ankle over his knee. "Even though I haven't seen my cousin in a while, we stay in touch. Matias knew I needed someone to take over the grounds keeping, and he recommended you. I don't know you, but I trust my cousin, and that's enough for me." He paused. "We all make mistakes. It's how we learn from them and move forward that proves our integrity. Do you still want the job?"

Afonso appreciated that Filipe was direct. "Yes, I do," he said slowly, trying to tamp down his eagerness. Afonso wanted this job more than he remembered wanting anything in his recent life. He would do his best to make sure he was worthy of that trust.

Filipe spent the next half hour going over a detailed list of each clearing stage, taking the time to answer all of Afonso's questions about the house and the property. He pulled out two sets of key rings. "This one has the keys to vehicles, including the one to the truck. You'll need to get supplies from town and haul equipment around the property. This ring has the keys to the house, the detached garage, and the outbuildings. There's a small house to the east side where the caretakers live. They pretty much came with the property when I bought it, and I didn't have the heart to kick them out. I restored their house and renewed their contract even though they're getting on with years and I'd rather they retire." He glanced at his watch. "I was going to introduce you, but I think they left already. The Silvas are only here between

Monday mornings and Friday afternoons, as they spend the weekends at their home in the village. Sometimes they have family who comes by, and then they drive down together."

Afonso nodded, adding another mental note to his list.

After all the instructions, including the location of the Wi-Fi tower and login information, Filipe presented two copies of a simple contract, which they both signed. Five months—from the last of May to the end of October—with an option to renew, if both parties agreed.

He handed Afonso a credit card. "All the expenses associated with the house and property are on this card. You don't have to worry about bookkeeping. I got someone for that."

Afonso resolved to keep all the receipts just in case.

"There's one more thing." Filipe paused and rubbed his chin. "I have a relative staying in the west wing." He indicated the area above them. "She's been here for a few weeks, and she's staying for as long as she wants or needs to." He reached for his wallet and drew out another card. "Anything she needs goes on this card."

Afonso hesitated. "Wouldn't it be better if she keeps the card herself?"

"She has a card of her own, but she's quite stubborn and doesn't drive. I usually take her lists when I go shopping as well. Just make sure she's got what she needs." After a pause, he added, "She was recently widowed and hasn't been ready to socialize much."

At first, Afonso thought of the woman in the old rose garden, but she was far too young to be widowed. His experience with older people was limited to the interactions he'd had with the ship's passengers, but he had observed plenty of stubbornness in that age range.

He took the card from Filipe. "I'll keep the receipts and send you digital copies."

Filipe looked at him. "Sure, that works. She's resting or I'd introduce you. Actually, it might be best to give her a wide berth until she's feeling better. Grieving has taken a toll on her, and she's been quite sick."

"Yes, of course."

"And she might need some rides to Castelo Branco, but you can hire somebody for that if you're too busy."

Afonso nodded, not knowing what to say until he knew the old lady better. "Do you have problems with villagers coming on the grounds?"

Filipe blew out a long breath. "It hasn't been a problem, since the house is a bit of stretch from the village. Just be firm, but kind, if you see anyone around who's not supposed to be here."

Afonso frowned. The mysterious woman must be a relative of the caretakers, visiting them for a few days. He was not looking forward to another confrontation with her. Hopefully they wouldn't cross paths again.

❄ ❄ ❄

Catarina leaned back against the stuffed chair in Filipe's bedroom as she watched him pack. "Say that again, please? I don't think I heard you right." Her mouth pressed into a hard line.

Filipe chuckled. "Don't start pouting, Catarina. That doesn't work on me. Besides, you knew I was looking for someone to take over the grounds before I leave." He shoved a few items of clothing into a day bag. "I should have hired someone two months ago."

She crossed her arms over her chest. "Do you really have to leave? I won't have anyone to talk to."

"Why didn't you call your mom like I suggested? Or one of your brothers? Or even a friend?"

She shook her head. "It's still too soon for that. I wouldn't want the media rags to get a clue on my maiden name." She hadn't used the Romano name in over six years. She was hiding in the district of Castelo Branco, hours away from Lisbon and from everything that had been her former life, hopefully far enough that no one would recognize her. Staying inside the property ensured nobody would. And even though Filipe was a high-profile business man, well known throughout the country, he'd never announced the purchase of the manor house. The remodel had been slow going as well, not attracting any attention beyond the few villages around the area. Any kind of attention was the last thing she wanted at this point in her life.

Filipe pulled the zipper closed. "You can always come with me."

"I can't." The less she was out and about the better, and the coast was more populated than this area.

"It's your choice, but I'll be away for a few weeks at least. The new guy I hired can get you anything you need, but you'll have to talk to him." He smoothed the traditional bedspread on the bed, then hoisted his bag. "I should have introduced you two before he left to the village."

"You hired him already? Did you even run a background check on him?"

"Yes, he's hired. Got the contract signed, the financial paperwork filled out, and he'll be around for at least five months." Filipe paused and looked pointedly at her. "And I did run a background check even though he was personally recommended by Matias."

Catarina wrinkled her forehead. "Matias who?"

Filipe arched an eyebrow in response. "Matias Romano. Our cousin. I know you've been away from the family scene for a while, but you remember Matias, don't you?"

Catarina ignored Filipe's remark. She carried enough guilt for keeping away from the family without needing reminders. "What room did you put him in?"

"I put him in the east wing, away from you. The guest bedroom facing the rear court."

"You gave him a room in the east wing?" For sure she'd run into the man even with him on the other side of the house.

Filipe looked up. "Should I have put him in the servants' quarters? Oh that's right, I don't have any." His mouth pressed in a straight line. "Don't be such a snob, Catarina. The attic is unfurnished, and the room off the kitchen is too small for someone staying this long."

Was she being a snob, or did she simply have a higher common sense?

"But you're leaving me with a stranger," she argued. How could he not see her point of view?

"The Silvas are here too."

"Not on the weekends."

Filipe gestured at the tablet sitting on the dresser. "Their phone number is on the list of important contacts. You can call them, and they'll be here in twenty minutes or less. Sete Fontes is not too far."

"It will still just be me and this guy in the house."

"I doubt you'll see him that much, with him so busy and you on the opposite side."

The farther from her, the better. "I'm not so sure about this new guy. I caught him watching me throw up by the rose bushes."

"You're still puking? I thought you were feeling better." Filipe opened the door, and they both exited the room.

She followed him to the landing. "So did I, but apparently not." She'd spent the last month and a half in close proximity to the bathrooms in the house. Today was the first day she'd ventured outside in a long time, and her moment of humiliation had been witnessed by a strange man. Just her luck.

Filipe stopped before descending. "Are you all right? You can't afford to lose any more weight. You should probably go to a doctor to see what's wrong with you."

Catarina sidled a hand over her still-flat belly and quickly moved it to her hip. "I'm pretty sure I'm on the mend." She could blame it on her little stowaway, even if she didn't tell Filipe. Kind of ironic that she'd finally lost the five kilos Juan-Carlos had nagged her about.

She flinched at the thought. Where had that come from? She didn't want to spare him any thoughts. He didn't deserve them.

Filipe watched her but didn't say anything. He probably regretted taking in a long-lost cousin who came with so much baggage. If Catarina had another choice, she'd take it, but she had nowhere else to go. She was much like the baby she carried: clandestine and totally dependent on someone else for the most basic needs.

They walked through the kitchen and stopped outside the back door.

Filipe playfully pulled a lock of her hair. "You take care of yourself, and don't get in too much trouble."

Catarina rolled her eyes. "You're just my cousin, not my older brother." The five-year gap between them had been more noticeable when they were children.

"I'm exactly the same age as Tiago. But maybe I'll call him instead." He smirked.

"Don't you dare." She leaned on the open jamb as he crossed the paved path to the rear courtyard toward the garage. "Are you taking the Audi or the Jeep?"

Filipe held up his keys. "The Jeep. Afonso has the keys to the Ford, and the Audi is there for you."

"Not funny," she called back to him.

Minutes later, the red jeep rolled out of the garage and Filipe waved at her. She held a hand up in return, unable to the hold back the small smile that pulled at the corners of her mouth when he honked the horn before disappearing around the house.

Catarina walked back to her bedroom. Two questions came to her mind. What was she going to do with herself without her cousin around?

And how was she going to avoid the man who'd just moved in?

CHAPTER TWO

$\mathscr{C}$atarina woke to her bedroom flooded in indirect light. This was the only suite in the house, with the bathroom, walk-in closet, and seating area to the right and the bedroom itself to the left, including a few windows facing west. The bed sat between the two walls. Through the large, naked panes, the sun's rays bounced on the pale gray walls and across the white coverlet.

She peeked at the digital clock on the bed side table and groaned at the late hour. Another morning spent in bed. This pregnancy sapped all her energy. She'd never been a morning person, but sleeping past eleven every morning was beyond her own standards. It didn't help that she'd gotten up twice during the night to go to the bathroom. Once she'd woken with the sounds of a distant piano, but she'd dismissed it as part of a weird dream and had fallen right back to sleep.

Her stomach grumbled, and she slipped a hand over it. At least, she'd remembered to place some Maria crackers in the bedside table drawer, as she'd read somewhere on the internet how it helped stave off nausea. Slowly, she opened the drawer and reached for the package. She took a bite from one and then stopped. How was she going to eat without leaving crumbs on the bed? Leaning over the edge of the bed, Catarina munched for a few minutes, hoping it would be enough. She'd deal with the crumbs on the floor later.

After a moment, she sat gingerly in bed, waiting for her stomach to rebel. When it didn't, she rose and approached the window overlooking the front yard. She unlatched the lock. Her eyes widened at the change: the sprouted grass was gone, now neatly mowed in a concentric pattern around the circle drive. On the wide lawn past the driveway, alternating rows of mowed grass marked the rectangular area bordering the old garden, which remained the same. But the hedgerows had been trimmed neatly, in wide contrast to the tangled mess of roses.

The new groundskeeper was keeping busy. Maybe Filipe was right and she wouldn't run into the guy after all.

As she got up to dress for the day, her stomach clenched, and she ran to the en suite bathroom. Fortunately, the vomiting didn't last long as she'd only had a couple of crackers. She brushed her teeth, then dressed in jeans and a loose top. For the time being, her wardrobe still fit.

Without the sounds of Filipe working on a project or playing music on his phone, the old house was quiet. The caretakers, Dona Madalena and Senhor Francisco, had left yesterday, as they usually did for the weekends. In the past few weeks since she'd arrived at Sunset Manor, Catarina had relied on Filipe to cook until Dona Madalena returned on Mondays. But now Catarina was on her own. The night before she'd fixed a frozen meal for dinner, but she'd barely picked at it. Having a personal chef on hand was one of the luxuries she missed. It was all in the past, and she'd do well to keep it there.

Catarina found clean dishes on the dish rack. The man had been in the kitchen to eat already. She'd heard him climb the stairs on his way to his bedroom in the evening yesterday but still hadn't seen him since their encounter in the old rose garden. Deep down, she was curious about him but not enough to seek him out. Nothing good would come of it.

Despite her lack of appetite, Catarina drew the carton of milk from the refrigerator and a roll from the freezer. After exactly ten seconds in the microwave, the roll was ready for a pat of butter. Maybe not the most nutritious breakfast, but with a weak stomach, she didn't dare eat anything heavier. She cut the prenatal vitamin in half and swallowed it carefully.

The vitamin container was fast approaching the one-third mark; she had maybe enough for two more weeks. Catarina sighed. She had to find a doctor in

Castelo Branco soon. And after, she'd have to find a way to get there without raising suspicions.

The rest of the day passed too slowly. She'd been relying on Filipe more than she'd noticed, and his absence was harder than she'd predicted. Reading, napping, and watching comedies on Filipe's tablet only filled part of the time, and the customary walk was out of the question as she didn't want to risk running into Filipe's groundskeeper. After rifling through some drawers in the kitchen, she found a lined spiral notebook and a pencil. It would have to do for now. She hadn't sketched in a while, but her fingers itched for something to do.

By the time she lifted her head from the paper, the sun slanted through the windows and changed the color of the walls into an almost-peach hue. She'd skipped an afternoon snack in favor of a few crackers again, but she'd have to venture downstairs for dinner.

The lights were on in the kitchen, and the most delicious smell permeated the air. Catarina paused to inhale. The smell was robust, full, and with a hint of spice, and her stomach grumbled. On the granite counter in the center island, a table for one had been set at the far end: a full plate, a bottle of dark beer, flatware, and a paper napkin.

There was no one in sight.

When her stomach grumbled one more time, Catarina approached the island where a platter with cubed roasted potatoes and asparagus spears sat to one end.

Despite the delicious smell, her weak stomach protested at the sight. How could she be hungry and queasy at the same time?

"You're welcome to join me for dinner."

Catarina yelped and jumped back.

A man stood by the glass sliding doors that led to the rear courtyard. The same man she'd seen yesterday.

❄ ❄ ❄

The woman's face turned scarlet. Had she been about to eat the food? She was the one he'd seen by the old rose garden. He walked toward the sink, and she took a step back. Afonso dropped the tongs at the bottom of the sink to be washed later and took the plate with the grilled steaks to the counter. What was she doing in the house anyway?

"Who let you in? Does Filipe know you're here?"

She frowned and crossed her arms. "Of course Filipe knows I'm here."

Her attitude and tone were not what he'd expected. She was too sure of herself. He quirked an eyebrow at her.

She looked away for a moment.

"I have an extra steak. Would you like to join me?" He repeated the invitation and motioned toward the plate.

Her cheeks pinked up in her otherwise pale face. "Thank you."

Was that a yes or a no?

Just in case, he set another place at the counter as she watched him warily. Now that he had a better look, there was something about her that hinted she might still not be feeling well. As pretty as she was, her low weight and fatigued expression had him wondering about her health.

Afonso turned away from her. It wasn't his job to judge her. Or think about how pretty she was. And he still didn't know anything about her.

He sat down and motioned for her to serve herself. "I'm Afonso Cortez, by the way. I was hired yesterday."

"Yes, you're the new groundskeeper." She sat, then placed potatoes and two asparagus spears onto her plate.

Afonso slid the bottle of beer in her direction, and she shook her head. "I don't drink," she said quickly.

He cut into the steak. "Are you going to tell me what you're doing here?"

"I came to get something to eat."

Ironically, she'd barely touched her food. "I don't mean here in the kitchen. I mean here in the house." He took a swig from his beer, trying to be less conspicuous in the way he watched her. "So you know my name and what I'm doing here, but all I know about you is that you're related to the caretakers."

She glanced in his direction. "Dona Madalena and Senhor Francisco?" Her eyebrows knit together in a show of obvious confusion. "Why would I be related to them? I'm Filipe's cousin."

Afonso stopped chewing. "He didn't mention any cousins. He said there was an old relative—" He stopped. "Are you the widow?"

She straightened in her seat and crossed her arms. "That's kind of rude to ask point-blank, don't you think?"

"Are you Filipe's widowed relative staying in the west wing?"

"I'd rather you don't refer to me as the widow."

In his mind, Afonso went through the conversation he'd had with Filipe yesterday. Filipe had never said his relative was an old lady. Afonso had assumed she was old since Filipe had said she was widowed. "I'm sorry. What's your name?"

"Catarina." She glanced at him. "Catarina Romano."

Afonso shook his head and almost laughed out loud. After the problems aboard the *Princess Catarina*, he'd had enough of Catarinas to last him a lifetime. And now he was living with one in a remote house.

"Are you laughing at me?" Her tone was decidedly not friendly.

"No." He was but not for the reasons she thought.

"I just saw you laughing. What do you have against me?"

"Not you in particular." He hesitated before going on. She'd probably think he was weird. "Just your name."

"Excuse me?" The incredulity and indignation in her voice were more apparent now.

Afonso shrugged. "The last Catarina I met didn't bring much luck." It was an understatement, but he didn't have to go into details.

"So does this aversion extend to other names or just mine?"

Afonso finished his steak. He was anxious to change the topic. With some luck, maybe she'd move on if he steered the conversation. "So you're Filipe's cousin? Are you Matias' cousin too?" She must be with the Romano last name.

Her expression remained guarded, but there was a hint of curiosity. "You've met Matias?"

"I have." Afonso wondered how much she knew about him. Was she aware the new groundskeeper had come straight from prison?

Afonso busied himself cleaning up while he decided what to do. She didn't say much and looked to be lost in her own thoughts for a little while, head down on her phone screen. He glanced at her, trying to assess her. What kind of woman was she? Being a Romano didn't mean she was as understanding as her male cousins. She looked to be a little younger than him, but he'd never been good at guessing a woman's age. She was pretty, but there was something about her—an uncertainty and sadness in her expression. Maybe it was the grief over her husband's death at such a young age that caused her to lose her appetite. Mourning and depression had a toll on physical health.

And why did she look so familiar? He was

certain he'd seen her before—not at the property, but somewhere else. "Have we met before?" When she scowled, he hurried on to explain. "I don't mean yesterday, or even here at the manor. Not recently."

"Is that your version of a pickup line?" Her voice let him know what she thought of it.

"What? No." This was not going well. He blew out a breath and turned to her. "I don't know how much Filipe told you about me, but I don't want to be accused of hiding my past."

She lifted her head toward him and frowned.

Afonso went on, not giving her a chance to say anything until he was done. "Due to some bad choices, I was in prison for the past few months. But I paid my debt, was released, and I'm not on probation. I'm here to work and do the job your cousin hired me to do. I'll stay out of your way, if you stay out of mine. It's a big house, and I'll be working outdoors most of the time, so I'm sure we can each keep to our own business. Nonetheless, Filipe said if you need anything to let me know." He walked over to the refrigerator and showed her the magnetic notepad and pen he'd found in a drawer earlier. "You can leave me a note on this pad, and I'll make sure to check on it. Since I get up early and you don't, it might be the best way to communicate."

She jumped to her feet. "Did you just call me lazy?" She stepped away from him, her arms straight at her side and her hands fisted.

This is what he'd feared. Afonso raised his hands. "No, I didn't call you lazy. I meant that you don't have to get up early, if you don't have a reason to. It's totally up to you." He grabbed the pad and pen from the refrigerator and set them down on the nearby counter. "You don't have to use these either. I'm sure you can find me if you need anything."

She didn't look any less angry. Maybe it was best not to say anything else tonight.

He walked past her. "Good night."

She stood in the same spot, arms crossed, watching him guardedly. Afonso made his way to his bedroom.

As long as she didn't complain to Filipe. Afonso couldn't lose this job.

❄ ❄ ❄

Find *Love Me At Sunset* on Amazon.

Portuguese Sweet Rice

This is a traditional Christmas dessert that has been converted to American measurements.
Prep time: 10 minutes
Cooking time: 20-30 minutes

Ingredients:

- 4 cups of water (with a good pinch of salt)
- 1 cup of short grain rice
- peel of one lemon
- 2-3 cinnamon sticks
- 3 cups of milk (whole or 2%)
- 1 cup of sugar
- 1 teaspoon of corn starch
- 3 egg yolks

ground cinnamon for decoration

Directions:

1. In a large pot, bring the water to a boil and add the rice, cinnamon sticks, and lemon peels.
2. After the water returns to a boil, let the rice cook for two minutes and add the milk.
3. Add the sugar after the milk boils.
4. Dissolve the corn starch in a little bit of cold water and add it to the pot.
5. Let it cook at a soft boil until the rice is tender.
6. Remove from heat and temper in the egg yolks, mixing them in slowly and stirring constantly.
7. Return to stove and cook on low heat, without boiling, for 3-4 minutes.
8. Remove the lemon peels and cinnamon sticks.
9. Pour onto individual bowls and decorate with ground cinnamon.

Enjoy it warm, at room temperature, or cold from the refrigerator. Refrigerate any leftovers.

THE AUTHOR

$\mathcal{L}$ucinda Whitney was born and raised in Portugal, where she received a Master's degree from the University of Minho in Braga, in Portuguese/English teaching.

She lives in northern Utah with her husband and four children. When she's not reading and writing, she can be found with a pair of knitting needles, or tending her herb garden.

She's the author of *The Secret Life of Daydreams* and *One Small Chance. Keep Me at Christmas* is the fourth book in her new *Romano Family* series.

Please visit her website at lucindawhitney.com for more information and news.